Freddy Meets
Carmen the Talking Mouse

By

Eva Roblins

ALSO BY EVA ROBLINS

Eva Roblins and the Enchanted Gate
- Book One: Return of the Princess

Gloves for José
- A Brief Tale of Love and Compassion

DEDICATION

In memory of Clarence Oren (Jimbo) Jr. (1926 -
1974), Signalman First Class, United States Navy, *USS
Nashville* (CL-43), Battle of Leyte Gulf, Republic of the
Philippines.

~~~

With unconditional love to the children, grandchildren, and great-grandchildren of Clarence Oren Jr.
May they feel a sense of pride in the true life account
of this story, as they join all Americans in honoring
those who commit the ultimate sacrifice for our great
nation.

~~~

To Ariell Alexis, Camryn Danielle, Chloe Lee, Emma
B. (Emmie), Emma Kate, Gabby Estefany, Jade, and
Lindsey Marie with love.

~~~

To my fellow redheaded pal, Ella Katherine with
freckled hugs and love.

Table of Contents

PREFACE

Clarence Oren Jr, aka Jimbo, was a legendary person, at least in my view. In the grand summation of humankind's history, Clarence's name is most likely nowhere to be found. All the same, he was a hero, a champion among champions. He was like all of the countless, anonymous brave men and women in uniform before, during, and after his life - a patriot. He answered the call to serve his country in her time of need. We owe him, limitless others, plus the brave men and women in uniform today a debt of gratitude. These brave heroes' unfailing dedication and willingness to commit the ultimate sacrifice defines us as Americans and keeps our nation free.

While this short story is predominately a work of fiction, some of its words are factual, historical truths of events that helped to win the peace in the Pacific

Theater during World War II. Jimbo's service onboard *USS Nashville* is one example, as are the mention of horrendous casualties resulting from the kamikaze attack on the ship. The movements by General Douglas MacArthur, Supreme Commander, Southwest Pacific Area (1880 - 1964) are also historical truths. Just like Jimbo, to whom this short story is dedicated, among others, General MacArthur was a true American hero. We owe the General a debt of thanks for his military genius and strategic vision that saved lives on both sides of the conflict. There are other truths contained in this work of fiction. They are included as a mark of respect to the memory of those who perished during the Second World War.

~~~

It is also important to talk about two characters mentioned in this story, Ariel-e and Camielle. These characters are based on likenesses of two wonderful youngsters - Ariell Alexis and Camryn Danielle. Ariell and Camryn's primary character likenesses, Ariel-e and Camielle, play key roles in my *Eva Roblins and the*

Enchanted Gate series of books. Finally, all others that I mention by name in the dedication also have primary character likenesses in my Enchanted Gate series of novels. Like Ariell and Camryn, I admire and love them all and offer them never-ending hugs.

~~~

"It is the soldier, not the reporter, who has given us freedom of the press. It is the soldier, not the poet, who has given us freedom of speech. It is the soldier, not the organizer, who has given us the freedom to demonstrate. It is the soldier, not the lawyer, who has given us the right to a fair trail. It is the soldier who salutes the flag, who serves under the flag, and whose coffin is draped by the flag, who allows the protester to burn the flag." - Father Denis O'Brien, USMC (1923 - 2002)

CHAPTER ONE

I AM NOT ALONE

Puppies

Kittens

Scaly green reptiles

Soaking wet stinky cedar chips

Floating goldfish corpses

Poop the world over

What a way to spend my Saturday!

These are Freddy's initial notions as he inhales unbelievably unpleasant scents and perceives unhappy sights of the caged animals before him. His mind races wildly.

Today is supposed to be my big day, my first day on the job - a real job. But will you look at all of these hungry, cooped-up animals? And will you smell that unpleasant smell! It's overwhelming! How can these poor animals stand it? All of them ought to be set free right here and now!

How would a human like it if he were caged? I seriously doubt that he would like it. I definitely wouldn't like it - not one bit. The air in this place is beyond doubt nasty, phooey, grotesquely stinky! Phew!

The day is rather young, a few minutes before seven o'clock in the morning at Lloyd's Pet Shoppe on the city's North Side. The morning sun is shining brightly through the Shoppe's gaily-decorated picture window. The picture window, like almost every inch of available wall space inside the Shoppe, is plastered with poster-sized reproductions of adorable animals. Most are of long-haired kittens and sweet-looking puppies.

Intermixed with the endearing cat and dog scenes are images of tiny white mice dashing through amber tunnels. There are posters of brightly colored finches, parakeets, and cockatiels happily perched in their cages. Various kinds of cheerful googly-eyed fish sporting big smiles swim playfully in schools. There are also smiling turtles and happy-go-lucky lizards of every shape and size imaginable.

Hither and thither hang posters of joyful hamsters, white mice, and joyful guinea pigs. They timidly peek from behind fun-looking, brightly-colored balls and spools of plastic yarn. Others seem to laugh as they scamper within upright whirling merry-go-rounds.

There are even a few posters of delightful furry ferrets and exotic non-poisonous snakes. Despite the posters depicting ferrets, Lloyd's Pet Shoppe no longer sells them. Mister Lloyd stopped selling ferrets after one bit him on the nose. He had to get five stitches.

As for the snakes, they're long gone as well. Freddy isn't completely sure what happened, but Mister Lloyd mentioned something about a snake escaping from its glass cage. Some of Freddy's friends once told him that the snake had slithered between the legs of an elderly lady patron which caused her to faint. Then, when another patron opened the front door, the snake slithered onto the street. It slid in the tall grass behind a fire hydrant and was never seen again. Freddy's friends always joke that the snake is lying in wait, ready to pounce without warning at passersby's on the sidewalk.

But for some odd reason, Mister Lloyd has a glass container that contains one single solitary snake. It's not real. It's made of rubber. Freddy presumes Mister Lloyd keeps the fake snake on display just in case somebody wants to order a live one. If so, there's a bigger pet shop across town that has all kinds of snakes. Mister Lloyd would probably have Freddy peddle his bike across town, fetch the snake the customer wanted, and then Mister Lloyd would sell it - at a huge profit no doubt.

Despite what should be a chipper looking scene in the Pet Shoppe on a Saturday morning, Freddy is in a gloomy mood. As we mentioned, he has just arrived at the Shoppe on this, his first day - the first genuine salaried job of his life!

All the same, he is utterly unprepared for the disturbing sights looming before him. He ponders if he's doing the right thing, being at the Pet Shoppe so early in the morning. He could be home sleeping!

Freddy glances at his watch and yawns. It is now one minute past seven o'clock. He thinks about his predicament.

I didn't know Lloyd's Pet Shoppe stinks this much before it opens for business. This place is a total disaster. All the cages and Plexiglass pens have gobs of foul-smelling poop in them. No wonder Mister Lloyd wanted me to report two and one-half hours before the Shoppe opens for business.

Freddy loathes physical work. Especially work that has anything to do with poop. He's probably no different than any other youngster his age. But Freddy knows he has to accept his fate. He has no other choice than to work.

He refuses to endure another long and boring, festive-deprived summer vacation. He needs money to nourish his voracious appetite for fun and food and frivolous things. Besides, he does not have a single good friend outside of the school. A summer vacation can be pretty boring without fun stuff to do and scrumptious goodies to eat and, certainly, no friends.

He consults his tattered black and white Composition notebook. The frown on his face speaks louder than words.

First, I have to exercise the puppies. Then I have to brush them and scrub their cages with Pine Sol. Afterward, I have to clean the kittens' litter boxes. After that, I need to change the reptile and rodents' bedding. Next, I have to scrape poop off of the birds' perches. Finally, I have to feed and water all of the animals. All of this should take me around two hours.

He looks around the Shoppe doubtfully. He refers to his notebook again to look on the next page. He slowly shakes his head with frustration.

Oh, I almost forgot. I have to remove the dead goldfish from the aquariums. To top it off, I have to clean up endless gobs of stinky poop all day long - all day long! Yuck!

Freddy understands cleaning up seemingly endless supplies of poop is the most important task he has as Mister Lloyd's trusted assistant. Mister Lloyd made that fact perfectly clear yesterday when he hired Freddy.

Mister Lloyd and Freddy were standing next to the puppy enclosures. Mister Lloyd had pointed to a recently deposited mound of doggy poop. He had said emphatically, "Freddy, customers will not buy animals and supplies from a Pet Shoppe when there's poop stinking up the place. Besides, mounds of poop here and there and poop smeared on bird perches are disgusting to look at. Therefore, Freddy my boy, your first priority is to clean up poop throughout the day."

Mister Lloyd had bent over with a paper towel in his hand to scoop up the boxer puppy's brand new mound of poop. He muttered, "Yes, Freddy my boy, I cannot put it more bluntly than this. Animal poop is a Pet Shoppe fact of life. In fact, poop is a fact of life for all living things. There's no getting around it. That's just the way it is."

With a hearty laugh, he had said, "Poop is everywhere, and it's here to stay. You tell me where there's no poop, and I'll tell you that you're lying."

With a puckered brow, Mister Lloyd had whispered as if someone might hear him, "Here in the Pet Shoppe, too much poop making cages smell repulsive results in disgusted and unsatisfied customers. Disgusted and unsatisfied customers results in the loss of revenue. And the loss of revenue results in letting my assistant go because I cannot afford to pay him. Do I make myself clear Freddy, my boy?"

As Freddy glanced around the store, he had managed a meek smile as he nodded his head in agreement. He had also pinched his nostrils with his fingers. That's because Mister Lloyd had waved the poop-filled paper towel mere inches from his nose.

As he remembers yesterday evening's scene, Freddy frowns once more.

On the other hand, I did not know then what I know now! I had no clue how dreadfully nasty a Pet Shoppe smells early in the morning. It smells *anti-*

antiseptic, like a polluted gas station bathroom on a desolate desert road. I should have told Mr. Lloyd to clean up his own poop and forget about me being his assistant. But, I need this job because I need money, lots of fun money. Besides, Papa would be very angry with me if I didn't stick to this job. So I'm stuck.

"This is going to be super gross!" Freddy exclaims out loud. "There are hungry animals, backbreaking tasks, and never-ending poop. Ugh! Today is going to be like a three-ring circus! What in the world am I doing here?"

"Oh, stop your complaining, mate!" a squeaky voice yells from the Shoppe's darkened depths. "If I were you, I would be thrilled to work here. At least you have a job and can roam freely throughout the Shoppe."

Freddy's eyes become the size of saucers as he freezes in his tracks.

I am not alone! Someone else is in the Shoppe! How can that be? I locked the back door when Mister Lloyd and I left last night during my training walk-through. I bolted the front door from the inside just minutes ago. I'm sure of it.

But wait! The voice I just heard sounded soft and meek. Perhaps it's a kid that's in here. We may have overlooked the kid last night when we closed the Shoppe. Gosh, I hope he's younger than me and not as strong!

Freddy grabs a broom from a nearby corner and slowly waves it in a threatening manner above his head.

"Who is that?" he yells. "What do you want? Come out where I can see you, or I'll smash your noggin with this broom! If Mister Lloyd knew you were here, he would give you a thrashing. You can bet your bottom dollar on that!"

"Can't do it, mate," the squeaky voice replies. "I cannot come out. I wish I could. Oh, how I wish I could come out!" He laughs and then in a singsong manner he says, "I would if I could, but I can't so I won't. I would if I could, but I can't so I won't. Ha-ha."

"You can and you will come out and you will show yourself!" Freddy stammers. "I got me a slingshot too. It's right here in my back pocket. I'm not afraid to use it either. You can bet your bottom dollar on that as well!"

"Wow, I'm truly scared now, mate," the unseen voice yells. "I bet you have yourself a fancy-dandy pocketknife, too. And I bet you go off like a frog in a sock. You're probably that crazy."

Freddy has no idea what it means *to go off like a frog in a sock*. But it doesn't sound like a flattering remark. What's more, he doesn't have a slingshot or a pocketknife, but he sees no harm in saying that he does.

His face set in a sneer, Freddy tells a fib as he says, "Matter of fact, I do have a pocketknife. And I have no problem using it as well."

"Well doesn't that just beat all!" the tiny voice murmurs sarcastically, "I am completely stoked! Is it one of those fancy Swiss knives with a fork, spoon, screwdriver, file, and a can opener? Maybe it even has a toothpick, huh? Or is it a cheap imitation, a stainless steel piece of junk made in some obscure country?"

Suddenly, the strange voice calls out to unseen others, "Hey mates, Freddy here has himself a fancy-dandy Swiss pocketknife. He has a broom and a slingshot to boot! I'm so sc-a-a-a-a-r-e-d!"

In response to the unseen voice's sarcastic scorn, a few squeaking giggles spring from sundry places within the dark recesses of the Shoppe's back rooms.

Now Freddy is very much alarmed.

Oh my goodness, there's more than one kid in Mister Lloyd's Shoppe! I'm outnumbered by a wide margin! I hope they don't ambush me!

He raises the broom high above his head and swings it in circles.

"Hey, you guys! I don't know who you are or how many of you there are for that matter. But, Mister Lloyd put me in charge. I'm his assistant so I'm pretty important around here. You better listen to me."

As he pushes his chest out, Freddy shouts, "Let me give you a word of advice because I know what

I'm talking about here. Mister Lloyd would be very upset if he knew you kids were hiding in his store. So why don't you just come out from wherever you are to face me? I'm not fooling around." As an afterthought he yells, "And I ain't scared of you either!"

Freddy reaches into his pocket with hopeful expectation that anyone watching will think he is retrieving a pocketknife. As he gropes in his pocket, all he feels are two marbles, a couple of pennies and a rubber band.

Telling a fib for a second time, he says, "Okay, I have my hand on my pocketknife. It's right here in my pocket. And my slingshot is in my back pocket like I said. Now, come out now, or I'll do some mightily bad bodily harm to all of you!"

"Hey Charlie," the squeaky voice laughs, "Didn't we hear that same line a while back in a movie we saw Down Under?"

"Aye, we sure did, mate," a second squeaky, but noticeably huskier, voice answers. "But I don't remember the name of the flick. Something with that good-looking Aussie in it I do believe. Some darned good acting, too. Course, it's an Aussie, so go figure."

Freddy is now beginning to get concerned as all-get-out. The second voice belongs to someone named Charlie. Charlie's voice is huskier than the first voice. Maybe teenagers or even adults are hiding in the Shoppe.

Freddy shudders.

If there are teenagers or adults here, my broom will be no match in the event of a showdown! I have to get out of here! I need to skedaddle right now!

Freddy starts to back away slowly. As he does, he shouts, "Now, show your faces, you cowards!"

"Hey, Charlie!" the first voice replies, "I thought I just informed our boy Freddy here I could not come out into the open. Did I not?"

"You sure did, Peter," Charlie replies.

Freddy glares at the floor as he rethinks the tight spot that he's in.

Okay, Peter and Charlie, Charlie and Peter. I now have two of their names. Perhaps they're friends. But, with more giggles somewhere in the shadows, I know for certain that Peter and Charlie aren't the only ones back there. Gosh, maybe they're robbers or something! And maybe they've got me surrounded. They might have blocked my escape through the front door!

I need to handle these guys very carefully. I'm outnumbered at least two to one, possibly many more to one. But with my broom, I should have a fighting chance. Not much of a chance, but it's better than nothing. I can whack a few of them with the broom handle. Then maybe I can make it to the door and get away. But I have to be ready to fight them if they decide to ambush me.

As he begins yet again to step back to the front door very slowly, Freddy says in a hesitant voice, "Say, Peter, tell me where you are so I can come to you. How would that be? I will not hurt you. I promise."

"Oh yeah, right, you won't hurt me!" Peter screams in a high-pitched voice. "At first, you were going to smack me with a broom. Next, you were going to take pleasure in doing some, and I quote, 'mightily bad bodily harm' to me with your fancy Swiss knife and slingshot. Now, you promise not to hurt me. You have serious double-talk, double personality problems, mate. You're also as mad as a meat-axe.'"

"I do not have a double personality! And I don't - I don't double-talk!" Freddy stammers. "And I'm not as mad as a meat-axe either, whatever in the world that is. You are!"

At this moment, Freddy is beginning to feel a wee bit braver since Peter seems worried that Freddy might hurt him. Despite his renewed bravery, Freddy notices that his knees are shaking. He also has shivers running up and down his spine. He may feel a little braver, but he's still scared.

With an authoritative voice, Freddy grumbles, "I just want to get on with my work. I have a ton of poop to clean. Can't you guys smell it? It's overpowering and a bunch of the stinkiness is coming from your area. It also smells like day old ammonia where you are as well."

With a grunt, he says with a sarcastic tone, "You guys should have used the bathroom. It's in the back room near the rear door. If you went to the bathroom on the floor, I'm not cleaning it up! You can bet your bottom dollar on that!"

Peter replies sarcastically, "Smell poop you ask? Heck, I'm sitting in a pile of poop right now, mate. And let me tell you something, *Mister I'm a really tough bigwig Pet Shoppe Assistant!* It does not smell like a bed of roses either if you know what I'm saying."

"Hey, Peter," Charlie cries softly, "Give it a burl. Why not tell him where you are? He won't hurt you. I bet he's just as afraid of Mister Lloyd as we are."

"Oh, do you really think so?" Peter asks. "It's easy for you to say, dimwit. You're a lot older than me. You're almost washed up too. I'm still in my prime. I have a lot more to lose than you. Furthermore, I have many more years to go, many more than you." He laughs.

"Who are you calling old - old and a dim - a dimwit, mate?" Charlie stammers defensively. "That's rubbish, Peter, and you know it. I may be older than you by a year or two, but I still have what it takes. You better watch your mouth, sonny. If you don't, I'll take that fancy Swiss knife and slingshot from Freddy and make you wish you never knew me." He laughs.

Freddy hears more laughter. These sounds of hilarity are new. They come from various places in the pitch-black back room. Now Freddy is more shocked and frightened than before.

There's a bunch of hooligans hiding in the Shoppe! But, how did they get in here? Wait! Wait a second! Peter mentioned *Down Under*. That refers to Australia. And those accents and totally weird phrases they're saying! These kids can't be local kids. I bet they're from Australia! Maybe they're lost or something. But how did they get in here of all places?

Then again, maybe they're part of an international pet-snatching ring! Perhaps they're trying to make trouble in Lloyd's Pet Shoppe! But why would they want to do that - and in this Pet Shoppe of all places?

There's a bigger pet store across town with loads more animals.

Freddy glances over his shoulder at the bolted front door. It's twenty or so feet away from where he is standing. If he turns to run now and runs as quickly as he can, he might have enough time to unbolt the door and escape. He will be safe, on the crowded, busy street long before Charlie and Peter, and their cohorts can reach him. He just might have enough time to break away from this madness!

CHAPTER TWO
DO YOU TRUST ME?

Freddy is in a sticky state of affairs. It is his first day on the job at Lloyd's Pet Shoppe. He has been having a discussion with two unknown something or others that have Australian accents. He is outnumbered at least two to one. Plus, he has heard laughter from others in the back room of the Shoppe.

Because of the laughter, he's pretty sure he's outnumbered many more to one. To make matters even more confusing, just as he is about to turn and run toward the bolted door, a third voice cries out from a cubbyhole to his immediate right.

"Hey, Freddy," cries the new voice. It is soft and soothing. This voice lacks the Australian accent.

"Do me a favor and lower your broom and pocket your knife and slingshot. Then move a bit closer. I want to get a glimpse of you in the overhead light if you please?"

"You're - you're a girl, aren't you?" Freddy sputters.

"I sure am, Freddy. My name is Carmen. I am Peter and Charlie's friend. Come now, be a love. Put away your weapons, and move into the light."

Like any other warm-blooded teenage boy his age, Freddy instantly feels at ease. The soft female voice resonates in his ears like a sugar-coated echo from a heavenly place somewhere within the Shoppe. He likes what he hears. He likes it a lot.

Freddy grins as his mind races.

This unknown person's voice sounds really sweet. By the sounds of her voice I bet she's a teenager. Maybe she's my age. I bet she's pretty, too. I sure could use a girl companion. I haven't had a female pal since Kathleen moved away last year.

"Okay, Carmen," he says, "I'm putting up my broom and pocketing my knife. I am moving into the light." He places the broom against the wall. Then he thrusts his hand into his pocket as he pretends to pocket the imaginary pocketknife.

Freddy moves a bit to his right. He glances at the ceiling. He is now standing directly beneath the fluorescent light fixture.

"Can you see me now?"

"Yes I can," the female's voice exclaims breathlessly. "I declare, Freddy, you are a good-looking boy, just as I expected. You truly are! Now take about five more itsy bitsy steps to your right so you will be able to see me. I am near the right-hand light switch on the wall.

"But first you'll have to turn on the light. It's quite dark in here as you can see. The light switch is in a little cubbyhole. It's behind a bunch of boxes. You'll have to grope for it. But be careful, the boxes are full of glass goldfish bowls. You do not want to break anything on your first day on the job. Mister Lloyd could fire you and that's the last thing that we want."

Thinking of Peter and Charlie, Freddy responds, "Okay, but I must warn you, Carmen. I still have my pocketknife and slingshot. Plus, the broom is well within my reach. Tell your two guy friends to stay cool. I don't want to have to beat them up or anything."

He clenches his right fist into a ball as he flexes his bicep. "I'm pretty tough as you can see."

Peter abruptly shouts at Carmen from the backroom to Freddy's left. Freddy instinctively spins around on his heels.

"See what I am saying, Carmen? I told you last night that you shouldn't trust this guy! He's going to do you harm. You can count on that! You better be ready to fight him! Get prepared to bite him with all your might and scratch him with your nails! Then pummel his large nose with your fists."

"Oh, be quiet, Peter," Carmen whispers annoyingly. "Freddy could not hurt a fly. I can sense it. Besides, why would he work in Mister Lloyd's Pet Shoppe if he harbored any ill feelings toward us?"

Suddenly, a dreadfully powerful voice bellows from the darkened room beyond the cubbyhole to

Freddy's right. The owner of this husky voice sounds really angry. Freddy steps back at least four steps. He recoils in terror as he spins around to face whatever it is that's yelling.

"I tell you, Carmen," the booming voice barks, "It's not right what you're doing! You could get hurt! I agree one hundred percent with Peter. It's not worth the risk, and you know it. So, stop your blabbering, Carmen. He'll never know who you are or where you are! Besides, he looks too stupid to figure it out by himself. So, don't encourage him to turn on the light! Maybe he'll just go away."

Then the voice growls at Freddy, "You just back away, Freddy! Back away before I get really angry and mess you up like the yellow-belly namby-pamby dolt you most certainly are!"

Freddy instinctively does what the voice tells him to do. As he backs away once more, he ponders the confusing dilemma he is now facing.

This is the fourth voice I've heard up to now! There are three guys and a girl. By the tone of his voice, this latest guy sounds really upset! He sounds like he's mean and a lot older than the others, too. Goodness, this store is crawling with some genuinely weird characters. And they're all hiding in the shadows. What in the devil am I doing? I'm getting out of here! I'm getting out of here right now!

He is just about to dash toward the front door when he hears Carmen's soft voice. She is pleading for him to stay.

"Freddy, no -, please do not leave, I beg of you! Do not fret about Brutus. He is protective. He's concerned I am talking to you that's all. Besides, he could not hurt you. He's an old and lonely, crippled creature that cannot walk without the aid of his cane. He does not know any other way to express himself.

"All he knows is how to act in the theater. He will not hurt you, Freddy. I promise. Now, please hurry over here and turn on the light so I can see you better and so you can see me. Please!"

Freddy hesitates for a moment, and then he does what Carmen asks. He walks to the cubbyhole to his right, feels for the switch in the dark and switches it on. The light's sudden, glaring intensity temporarily blinds him. Once his eyes adjust to the harsh brightness, and he sees what Carmen is, he continues to blink his eyes rapidly with uncertainty.

Holy cow! I can't believe what my eyes are seeing! If my eyes are not deceiving me, and the female voice is, in fact, coming from her, Carmen is a mouse! She's a reddish-brown mouse. She's the one that has been talking to me! What is happening here? Was a mouse really talking to me? Naw - that's impossible!

But it has to be the mouse that was talking to me. There is no one or anything else in this little cubbyhole. There's just this little mouse inside her Plexiglass enclosure. And wow - this mouse is totally cool, and she's cute too!

Freddy is not imagining things. Carmen *is* a mouse. She is standing on her hind legs as she places her front paws for balance on the Plexiglass wall. She is in good spirits with a huge smile on her face.

Carmen has silky red hair that rests on the top of her wee-bit mouse head. She also has a pretty, reddish-brown face surrounded by reddish-brown whiskers. In fact, except for her red hair, her entire body is reddish-brown.

Her slightly slanted dark blue eyes are captivating, their oval spheres encircled by long, russet-colored eyelashes. The lashes seem to dance the foxtrot when she smiles. She has a small mole on her left cheek that attractively emphasizes an alluring dimple.

Carmen has painted her voluptuous lips in the softest red hue imaginable. She is much larger than other mice Freddy has seen. She has a slender, shapely body, almost like that of a human female adult, except with distinct mouse features. Without a shred of doubt, Carmen is the most elegant and beautiful mouse that has ever scurried across the Earth. She stares lovingly into Freddy's eyes for the longest time.

Freddy is too moved to speak. It is as if he is hypnotized. He can feel his face is flushed and his ears are hot with awkwardness. After what seems like forever, he shakes his head as he rapidly blinks his eyes with disbelief.

He declares in a whisper, "Why, you're a mouse!" You're a beautiful talking mouse! But that's impossible. Mice can't talk. And you're different than most mice as well. I have never seen a mouse that is anything other than brown, gray or white. You are like reddish-brown from head to toe. And will you look at that? You also have red hair on the top of your head. You are wearing a dress, too. This is hard to believe!"

Actually, what Carmen is wearing is a skirt. It is pink. A pattern of tiny white hearts is scattered on it. Her matching short-sleeve blouse is also pink.

"You are quite wrong, darling," Carmen declares bluntly. "Some mice do talk. I am proof of that. Peter, Charlie, and Brutus also provide proof that mice can talk. There are others here in the Shoppe that can also talk. However, they are shyer than the four of us. Yes, Freddie, we are talking mice. But, there is no time for that now. Hurry and open my cage, darling. Please!"

"Hey, don't you do it, Freddy Ole Boy!" Brutus brusquely shouts. "Don't you dare open her cage! I don't care what the others say. I don't trust you! If I weren't in this Plexiglass pen, I would smack you senseless with my cane you, you, you stupid human you!"

Freddy merely smiles as he sees Brutus at last. He is in a small wire cage to Carmen's right. Brutus is a hunched-back elderly brown mouse. He is standing on his hind quarters, holding onto the wire mesh with his left paw. A gnarled wooden cane is in his right paw. The cane seems to keep him from teetering backward onto the shredded newspaper.

Brutus is wearing a black tuxedo, long-sleeved white shirt, and an oversized red bow tie. A tattered gray top hat adorns his head. Although he is a dark brown mouse, his whiskers are gray. His deep brown eyes are staring intently into Freddy's wide-open eyes. He is glowering at Freddy.

"Brutus, please watch your manners!" Carmen suddenly scolds as she turns to her right to glare at

Brutus. "I do not care to hear another thunderous word out of your heartless mouth unless it is to say something considerate and gracious to our friend here. You apologize to Freddy. You apologize to him right this instant! Do I make myself clear, Brutus?"

Carmen crosses her arms in front of her as she glares at Brutus. Freddy notices she is rapidly drumming her right hind paw up and down. She's obviously very much annoyed.

Brutus lowers his head in shame, saying, "Yes, ma'am, you certainly do make yourself clear. Please accept my apologies, ma'am."

Carmen nods her head in approval as Brutus turns away to sulk in the rear of his enclosure.

Brutus says meekly, "You're right, of course, too. I say again, I'm sorry, Carmen, dreadfully sorry." Addressing Freddy as he glances over his shoulder, he murmurs, "Sorry, mate, I'm really sorry. No harm was done I hope."

"No problem, Brutus," Freddy replies with a timid smile. "It is quite okay, dude, I mean, mate."

Freddy's face suddenly brightens.

Wow! I take back what I said moments ago. Today is turning out to be rather awesome after all. Carmen definitely commands respect from the other mice in the Shoppe. It is quite obvious that she is the one that is in charge around here. She's one tough cookie, no doubt about it. I like her a lot.

Freddy quickly shakes his head as he continues to stare at Carmen. He whispers, "But, what in the world am I saying? I am having a conversation with mice!"

With a giggle, Carmen softly says, "Yes you are, Freddy, you most certainly are." Glancing over her shoulder at Brutus, she adds, "Please ignore Brutus when he gets angry. He is such a dear despite his mulish ways. He is forever and a day looking out for me. He loves me and I love him too. But he can sometimes be very annoying as you've just witnessed."

Changing the subject she pleads, "Come now, and why not unfasten this door so I can get a better look at you? Seeing things plainly through this cloudy Plexiglass enclosure is impossible to say the least."

Freddy replies, "You will not try to escape, will you?" His voice contains a hint of uncertainty.

"Do not be ridiculous. Why would I try to escape? I have no place to go. Besides, I would not do anything to get you in trouble. Please be a dear, Freddy and unlock my door."

Freddy unlocks the tiny Plexiglass door. Carmen pushes it wide open. Then she stares at him for the longest time, her eyes unblinking. Finally, she exclaims, "Oh, my goodness, Freddy, you surely are good-looking. No wonder Mister Lloyd hired you. You will be good for business. I don't doubt it one bit."

Taking a long deep breath, she adds, "I dare say, Freddy, will you smell that air! This is the first time I have had fresh air on my whiskers since I arrived. This stifling Plexiglass enclosure can be restrictive even with its air holes. It doesn't breathe properly and it gets all steamy inside. Plus it smells too. Thank you very much, my dear."

Freddy closes his eyes as he massages his temples. Still disbelieving what is happening, he shakes his head for the umpteenth time. After he opens his eyes, he stammers, "You are welcome, Carmen. I apologize for appearing to be shocked. It's just that I am not accustomed to hearing mice talk. You mice are my first."

"Oh, do not let it trouble you, Freddy," Carmen says. "Of the few people in the world of humans who have heard us talk, none will ever admit it. They would not dare. Others would think that they were crazy or hallucinating, do you not agree?"

"Yes, I imagine people would think such a thing," Freddy admits. "So how did you mice learn to talk?"

"Well, in Australia there are millions more mice than anywhere in the world. During certain times of the year, mice crawl over one another. They emerge out of cupboards, basements, mouse holes, cracks in the ground, all sorts of places. There is a mad quest for food. I dare say mice drive the Aussies nuts. There are so many of us in one place among the human population in Australia. It was inevitable over time that a few of us would have learned to talk.

"In fact, I have this youngster human friend in Australia with whom I talk quite frequently. Her name is Ariel-e. She can dance, and sing and wow! Is she ever a very talented actress! She's also incredibly pretty, Freddy. I'm sure you would like her.

"At any rate, she and I talk all the time in person whenever I visit my relatives Down Under. I sometimes talk with her on the phone when I'm traveling abroad as well. But we don't talk too often because long distance charges are truly expensive."

She laughs, "Besides, it's very difficult for me to call her. I don't own a phone." She does a little side-step jig saying, "It's also hard to jump around on all those little numbers to dial the phone. I'm forever and a day tripping over my own two hind paws and getting a wrong number." She giggles.

"But, how could that happen?" Freddy asks. "I mean, how did you evolve to talk when others did not?"

"Oh, that is an easy question to answer. Our ancestors simply had more exposure to humans than most mice. My ancestors, in particular, had a very nice friend who spent hours talking to them each and every night. He's actually the one that taught my ancestors how to converse. He also taught them how to act properly around humans. The brown mice in Mr. Lloyd's Pet Shoppe have had a lot of experience in this regard as well. We're not a nuisance like other brown mice. We have etiquette." Carmen executes a stylishly graceful curtsy.

"You see, Freddy, the others are members of a traveling troupe, a cabaret of sorts. They dance and perform in theaters. Some of them sing as well. Every brown mouse in this store is an actor, except for me of course. I am probably the only reddish-brown female mouse in the entire world with scarlet hair on the top of her head." She laughs exuberantly. "Even so, I do not act. I am a super clumsy klutz on the stage." She does another sidestep as she pretends to trip over her own two hind paws.

As she stretches on her hind legs, she says, "The mice of the troupe usually perform tricks in group settings that resemble plays. They talk and sing as well, but only when performing for other mice, never in front of humans. The troupe plays in the finest cities. They eat the most delicious gourmet foods. And they sip the most luscious, vintage fruit juices the world has to offer.

"Audiences greet the troupe warmly and with respectful applause everywhere it goes. The troupe's human handlers treat the mice agreeably as well. I must confess, however, that people treat white mice better than us brown mice, but we make out okay. Despite the troupe's special gifts, they, like me, make it a rule to never, ever talk to adult human strangers. We sometimes talk to human children, but never adults."

"Why don't you talk to human adults?" Freddy asks. "It would seem having the ability to talk to human adults would make you mice even more popular."

"Perhaps," Carmen says. "However, there are no guarantees. Unscrupulous humans may try to exploit us. Human scientists may try to perform hideous experiments on us to find out why it is that we can talk."

"Oh, I don't think that would happen," Freddy replies. "If I were a scientist, I would try to make you happy. I would also try to breed as many talking mice as possible. It would be pretty cool to have a world full of talking mice." He smiles.

"Could you imagine? All the lonely kids in the world would have a playmate right there in their pockets. They would have something in which they could confide at any time, day or night. Do you see what I mean?"

"Yes, I do see what you mean, Freddy," Carmen sighs. "Nevertheless, humans are notorious for conducting ruthless experiments on animals, particularly on mice. I am afraid the track record for humans is not too attractive in this regard. Human beings have even conducted experiments on other humans. Do you know what some doctors and scientists did to innocent human victims during World War II?"

"I sure do," Freddy replies. "They conducted shocking experiments on people. It was terrible. I read about the incidents in one of my Papa's books that focused on World War II. But that was very long ago, Carmen, way back during the Second World War. I don't think humans would allow a repeat of that practice. Do you?"

"Maybe, maybe not," Carmen says. "At least I hope not. However, humans are frightened by mice for some strange reason, especially brown mice. Women scream and jump on chairs when they see us. Men and boys bait us with traps, shoot at us with pellet guns, and run after us with brooms, sticks, and throw stones.

"Hardware and grocery stores sell mice poisons and mouse traps like they were candy. Field mice are mistreated, especially in the more urban areas. No, Freddy, I do not think that it is wise to let adult humans know we can talk."

Freddy nods his head and says, "Yes when you put it that way, I guess you are right. Why then, Carmen, are you talking to me?"

"That is positively an excellent question, Freddy!" Carmen exclaims. She jumps out of her enclosure onto the counter.

"To be honest with you, the brown mice and I had a meeting last night. You were the primary topic of the gathering. Let me tell you, there was quite a commotion during the gathering.

"Some of the mice, like Brutus and Peter, do not trust you. But the majority of the mice, to include Charlie and me, well, we think we can trust you. Since we know that today is your first day on the job, it seems like today is the best day to establish an understanding with you. So, here we are Freddy, talking to each other. From my standpoint, it is an exciting experience. Wouldn't you agree?"

"Hello, Carmen. Oh, darling? Remember me, hmm?"

That's Peter's voice! I almost forgot he was here!

"Is Freddy taking pleasure in plotting to hurt you, honey?" Peter says. "Or are you two lovebirds conspiring to send the rest of us back to Australia?"

"Peter, you know, you can be a real pain sometimes!" Carmen scolds. "You're just jealous and angry with me because I won't be your girlfriend. What's more, Freddy is a nice kid. You know that. How can we get him to help us if we accuse him of doing something when he is not?"

Freddy is now very frightened. He did not agree to help anyone or, more correctly, these mice!

"'Wait a minute here, Carmen," he cries. "What do you mean by, 'how can we get him to help us?' You mice are not going to ask me to help you escape or do anything illegal, are you? You're not going to ask me to do something that will get me in trouble with Mister Lloyd, are you?'"

The look on Carmen's whiskered face is one of complete surprise. "Freddy darling, don't be silly. I would never ask you to do something that would get you in trouble. What I have in mind is nothing sinister."

She lowers her head and pouts, and then she whispers softly, "It gives me much pain to know that you would assume someone as sweet as me would even consider such a thing."

She looks up at Freddy, her eyelids blinking rapidly. Her beautiful blue eyes look quite sad. By the look on her face, it appears as if she's about to burst into tears.

"Okay, I am sorry, Carmen. I trust you, I honestly do. But tell me what is it you want me to do. However, whatever it is, I think we better do it quickly. I have to attend to all of the animals."

Freddy frowns and with a sigh he says, "And then I have to clean up this nasty, foul-smelling poop all day long."

"That attitude is much better, Freddy," Carmen says with a radiant smile. "Friends should trust one another. We *are* friends, are we not?"

"Of course we are," Freddy states matter-of-factly. "On the other hand, how do I know you will not go back on your word? I want to trust you, Carmen. I honestly do. But, what guarantees are there?"

"There are no guarantees in life, sweetheart," Carmen says with a smile. "Trust your instincts. Trust me as a true friend trusts another friend, okay? Now slide your hand toward me, palm up so I can jump onto it."

"Okay, but promise you will not try to escape?"

In reply to Freddy's question, Carmen snaps to attention. She crosses her heart with her tiny right paw. Then she holds her left paw in the air as if she is taking a solemn oath. She says, "I swear."

It is then Freddy notices her tiny nails. She has tinted her nails with a hint of emerald nail polish.

Freddy also notices Carmen is wearing a small heart-shaped medallion around her neck that is suspended from a gold chain. The medallion is purple with white borders on either side. It thumps carelessly against her blouse as she rises to jump onto Freddy's outstretched palm. For some strange reason, the medallion looks vaguely familiar to him. He thinks to himself that he's seen a picture somewhere of a similar medallion. Now another thought crosses his mind.

Carmen had crossed her heart with her right paw. That's okay. But she held her left paw up high in the air when she pretended to take an oath and said, "I swear." Was she trying to trick me? Um, maybe she wasn't. Perhaps that's the way mice take oaths, with their left paw held high instead of their right.

"Oh, Freddy, darling, I thank you!" Carmen exclaims. She is smoothing her skirt as she stands on her hind legs in Freddy's palm.

"You are a loyal friend, Freddy. Thank you for trusting me. Mister Lloyd has one super-awesome worthy assistant!"

Freddy stares at his watch. Mister Lloyd? Nine-thirty! Oh no!

"Goodness!" Freddy shouts out loud, visibly startling Carmen. "I have less than two hours to get this place cleaned up before Mister Lloyd gets here. It will take me more than an hour just to remove the poop from the cages!" He looks at the floor miserably.

"You have plenty of time, Freddy," Carmen offers reassuringly. "Trust me. We will help you. We know how to attend to all of the animals. We are also quite skilled when it comes to cleaning up poop, despite how intolerable a task it may appear to be."

Freddie looks at her quizzically. Seeing his questioning look, Carmen giggles.

She sure does look cute when she laughs. I love her little dimple! And who would have thought a mouse would be wearing clothes? Plus she has painted nails and lipstick too.

"I bet you are wondering how it is that we know how to clean up poop, "Carmen asks.

Freddy nods his head slowly.

"To be perfectly blunt," she says, "when humans put us in Plexiglass pens or lock us behind bars, they often ignore clear-cut decency. They neglect to change our bedding twice a day. We are forced to live in our droppings for days, sometimes weeks on end. Humans apparently do not think we are bothered by the vulgarity of it all, although we truly are."

With a frown she says, "Too much poop is an acute problem when we are being transported from one place to another. It is absolutely disgusting and extremely unsanitary. Please trust me when I say we know how to clean up poop. It is our number one priority for self-preservation; that is, after eating and sleeping and exercising on our little merry-go-round wheels." She laughs.

Freddy laughs in response saying, "I bet you are an expert at cleaning up poop. Can you really help me, Carmen? If so, how can you help me?"

"Freddy, all you have to do is put your trust in my friends and me," Carmen replies. "The other mice and I will do all of the work." She bats her eyelashes a few times and inquires, "Do you trust me, Freddy?"

"Yes, Carmen, I trust you," Freddy says. "Please tell me your plan and what you want me to do in return."

Carmen asks Freddy to raise his upturned palm toward his face until her head is about six inches from his nose. When his palm is in the right position, she smiles deviously. She wants to get up on her tippy toes to lean forward and plant a kiss on Freddy's nose, but she thinks better of it.

She now has his undivided attention as she stands a half-foot from his nose. She casually purses her tiny lips. Then she makes a barely inaudible smacking sound as she blows him a loving, sweet kiss with her left paw.

Freddy is instantly stunned. He is also embarrassed by Carmen's touching display of affection. His face turns bright red. Carmen laughs loudly at his reaction.

Carmen asks Freddy to move his palm to the right side of his head so she can whisper in his ear. When his palm is sufficiently close to his ear, she clumsily stretches her hind legs and gently rests her front legs against his ear lobe.

Her furry cheeks touch Freddy's ear. This causes him to tremble involuntarily. Then his hand begins to shake as a shiver moves down his arm across his back to his spine. He starts giggling.

Carmen just about loses her balance. She's teetering on her hind legs as she desperately holds onto Freddy's ear lobe.

"Careful, Freddy," she warns. "Otherwise, I will slide away from your jiggling palm to land rump first onto the hard linoleum floor!"

"Oh, sorry," he sighs. "Your whiskers tickled me. They caused shivers and I could not help but laugh."

Now, unbeknownst to Freddy, Carmen's face is very serious-looking as she whispers into his ear. Her tiny front paws are gesturing persuasively. She also crosses two of her claws on her left paw, as if she is making a desperate, silent wish. A serious issue is obviously at stake from Carmen's perspective. There is no doubt about it.

As Freddy listens, his face slowly transforms from a look of curiosity to a look of unease. Next, his face turns to one of instantly recognizable displeasure. He exclaims forcefully, "Oh, Carmen, I cannot possibly do that!"

Freddy's sudden outburst catches Carmen by surprise. She is off-balance in a flash. Her tiny paws try to claw frantically at something, anything. She reaches out with her front paws to grab onto Freddy's ear to keep from falling. But she is unable to grab it. With her front appendages futilely flailing in the air, Carmen quickly loses her balance. She stumbles backward and falls on her rump onto Freddy's palm with a loud *thump!*

"Ouch! That smarts!" she cries out softly.

Freddy is alarmed. Carmen could have injured herself!

He quickly brings his palm in front of him until it is a foot or so from his chest. He looks down to see that Carmen is sitting on her haunches. Thankfully, she is unhurt.

She appears to be quite ill at ease from her fall. She is grim-faced. What Freddy sees next is incredibly humorous. It is also unforgettable.

Clearly, Carmen is annoyed and embarrassed. To show her displeasure for having fallen rump first onto

Freddy's palm, she angrily stares at Freddy for the longest time. Then she fearlessly folds her tiny front legs across her chest. She exhales an ear-splitting, high-pitched, "Humph!" Then she purposely turns her head to the side as she looks away indifferently.

Freddy cannot help but smile at Carmen's display of rebelliousness. It is safe to do so since she is looking the other way.

Wow! She's very angry with me, but I simply cannot do what she asks. It's not worth the risk!

Finally, after what feels like forever to Freddy, Carmen slowly turns her head to look at him. She focuses her blue eyes to stare intently into his. When Freddy does not react, she tilts her head to one side. She is inviting him to explain his recent outburst and denial of her request. She also taps her right hind paw over and over as she impatiently waits for his reply. Her front legs are still folded across her chest. She's totally ticked off.

"I'm sorry I startled you, Carmen," Freddy says with a timid smile. "And I'm really glad you're not hurt. But what if Mister Lloyd finds out? He will fire me for sure. No, Carmen, I cannot do it. I won't!"

Carmen slowly rises from her sitting position. She stands on her hind legs. She places her front legs by her sides. Then she turns her furry paws up. With this non-verbal expression, she is asking Freddy to provide further justification. She once more looks as if she is ready to cry.

"No, Carmen," Freddy stammers, "I don't think I can do it. I honestly don't."

Carmen returns to her sitting position on Freddy's palm. She rests her tiny paws on her slender out-stretched legs. She smoothes the creases in her skirt. "Please?" she implores.

Now tears are starting to flow from her cheerless eyes. The sudden wetness begins to stain her reddish-brown furry cheeks. She hangs her head and pouts.

Freddy slowly nods his head back and forth. However, his position is now tentative, to some extent undecided. For sure he feels awful.

Carmen places her tiny paws into a prayer-like gesture in front of her painted lips. She looks up and says, "Please, Freddy, I beg of you. Please. All you have to do is open his desk, remove the items, and bring them to me. I will have them for fifteen minutes at the most. I promise. Then you can put them back into Mister Lloyd's desk. He will not even know you touched them. You will be borrowing them for a few moments, not stealing them. What harm is there in that?"

"None, I guess," Freddy replies somberly. "However, Mister Lloyd may know I was in his office. He will know I rummaged in his desk. He told me his office was strictly off-limits. I could get fired, Carmen!"

"He will never know you were in his office," Carmen implores. "I have been observing him for some time now. He will be so impressed with your work after we mice clean the Shoppe, I bet he will not even notice. Trust me, okay? I am begging you,

Freddy. Please?" Then, as she once again blinks her eyelids rapidly, she whispers, "Friend?"

Freddy takes a moment to think it over. He finally responds, "Well, okay, Carmen. I will take the risk, but only this one time. Please do not ask me to do anything else that could get me fired. I do hope you understand, yes?"

"Of course I do, darling," Carmen says with a timid grin. "And I thank you from the bottom of my heart."

She suddenly stands. She once again smoothes the creases in her skirt and says, "Freddy, I know everything about you and your family. However, you know nothing about me. Hence, before we begin with our plan, I want to tell you a story. It will give you more information about me and my friends. It will take but a few minutes. We have plenty of time."

Freddy scratches his head. How can she know about my family and me? Oh well, we can cross that bridge when it is necessary to cross it.

He takes a quick look at his watch. Then nodding his head in agreement he says, "All right, Carmen, but please be quick. We only have a few minutes to spare, okay?"

"Okay, darling," Carmen replies. "Now pull up a stool and listen very carefully if you please. The story I am about to tell you is one of the most remarkable stories you will ever hear. It will probably be the most memorable as well, one that you'll tell your children's children."

CHAPTER THREE
JIMBO LOVED HIS PETS

Freddy has just pulled up a wooden stool. He is sitting on it with his long legs splayed before him. He smiles as Carmen sits down at eye level on the shelf beside him. She closes her eyes as she begins to narrate her story.

"My story starts in the Philippines. All of the brown mice Mister Lloyd has in this store are descendants of mice born in the Philippines. Despite my heritage, however, I am an American. Los Angeles is my place of birth.

"All through World War II Philippine mice, along with nearly every other species of rodents on the tropical archipelagos were persecuted to the brink of extinction. That was understandable. Rodents were near the bottom of the food chain. We still are when you think about it.

"The war was a terrible ordeal for everyone involved. Famine and wholesale atrocities contrary to human dignity were rampant. Many human natives of the islands, to include innocent women and children, perished in the fighting.

"The war also took its toll on Allied and Japanese troops. Atrocities were committed on both sides, by both Japanese and Allied Forces. But the troops were simply following orders of their superiors. All the same, the troops and countless millions of innocents were caught in the crossfire of human misfortune. It was a dark period in the history of mankind.

"As far as I can figure, my ancestors were born in the back room of a small sari-sari store in a place called Bataan. Bataan is on the largest island in the Philippines. The island is called Luzon.

"Like the human population, mice suffered during the War. There was little food. Bataan was also the scene of wholesale suffering by American and Allied troops. It was the site where the infamous Death March occurred. At least seven thousand American and Filipino soldiers of the 70,000 that had been taken prisoner perished during the Death March."

"You know what, Carmen?" Freddy interrupts excitedly. "My Grandfather served onboard *USS Nashville* during World War II. It was a heavily armed cruiser. It was the flagship of General Douglas MacArthur. The General had vowed, when he left the Philippines, 'I shall return.' The *Nashville* carried the General back to the Philippines. Then the ship was guarding the Straits during the Battle of Leyte Gulf. My Papa told me all about it. He told me about the Death March too!'"

"I know, Freddy," Carmen responds.

"But how do you know that?" Freddy asks. "How could you know my Grandfather served in the Philippines area of operations?"

"Oh, it is not important how I know," Carmen says with a smile. "But I know. You were saying?"

Freddy says, "Yes, right. My Grandfather was injured quite severely when a Japanese kamikaze plane hit *Nashville*. He almost died. He had just turned eighteen a few months before. He enlisted in the Navy at seventeen. It seems that he lied about his age. He was a big fellow. I guess that's how he enlisted when he was still not legally old enough to join the Navy."

Carmen nods her head. She gestures with her paw for Freddy to continue.

"My Papa told me Grandpa nearly lost his leg, and his entire chin was severely injured. He required extensive plastic surgery to restore his chin. He had to undergo many skin grafts. He also had a four-inch piece of shrapnel embedded in his lower abdomen. Of course, they removed it. All the same, that's what caused him to limp for the rest of his life.

"As a result of his injuries, Grandpa endured many painful operations. He couldn't eat solid foods for many months. He had to get his nourishment through a straw. He lost a lot of weight, which for a novice boxer in a boxing ring was a big deal. He couldn't talk for the longest time. He also had nearly a year of rehabilitation, just so he could walk somewhat normally. His wounds were terrible. They haunted him for the rest of his life.

"My Papa once told me a story when, as a teenager, he watched as my Grandpa stood in front of the bathroom mirror. Grandpa was removing a bit of tiny iron shrapnel from his face, neck, and upper chest with a set of tweezers. He would use a strong magnet and magnifying glass to find the shards of metal embedded beneath his skin. That was nearly twenty years after the war!

"My Grandpa also caught malaria in the tropics. He would often spend sleepless nights shivering in his bed. He had lots of nightmares too. We didn't know what it was called back then, but he suffered from Post Trauma Stress. My Grandma told me that my Grandpa often woke up in the middle of the night very afraid. He passed away young, at forty-eight years old. I guess his war wounds had finally caught up with him."

Freddy is looking down at the floor. Tears are in his eyes. He whispers, "Yes, fighting is terrible and I wish there weren't any more wars. But I'm thankful brave men and women are willing to fight when called upon to do so." Freddy looks up at Carmen and says, "Otherwise how could we be free?"

Then, with a puzzled look on his face, Freddy says, "Regardless of Grandpa's closeness to Luzon, I doubt if any of your relatives on the northern islands knew him. He was on the southern islands for only a couple of weeks. After he had recuperated sufficiently to travel, he sailed on a transport ship back to the United States. He was in pretty bad shape. He had almost died as I said. I'm glad he didn't. Otherwise, I wouldn't be here."

Carmen looks at Freddy, her face full of sadness. She is teary-eyed. She says softly, "I see, Freddy. I am truly sorry. I am truly sorry your Grandfather suffered so much. I know he was a decent man, a brave man."

"It's okay, Carmen," Freddy replies. "I apologize for interrupting. Please continue with your story."

Carmen clears her throat as she tries to regain her composure. "As I was saying, famine was rampant in the Philippines during the War. Women and children and the elderly were particularly vulnerable. They were suffering very badly. The food was scarce. As a result, most of my ancestors' friends and relatives perished during a terrible episode called the Mouse Purge. Thank goodness my ancestors survived or, obviously, like you, I would not be here today.

"The chances of outliving the conflict seemed bleak for my ancestors during the War. Then one day a friend visited my ancestors in the middle of the night. He lived on Corregidor Island. He told them about a secret plan he overheard while searching for food in Corregidor's Malita Tunnel.

"He had heard that the President of the United States, Franklin Roosevelt, was trying to convince General MacArthur to leave the Philippines at his earliest opportunity. The President wanted the General to lead Allied troops on the offensive in the Pacific. The General was a true hero and a great man.

As a result, the General did not want to go and leave his troops behind, fifteen thousand of them."

"I read about Corregidor," Freddy says in earnest. "It was MacArthur's Headquarters in the middle of Manila Bay after he evacuated the city of Manila. Am I correct?"

"You are correct, Freddy," Carmen says. "Corregidor was believed to be invincible. The Japanese had overrun Luzon and established a naval blockade of Manila Harbor. It was soon apparent that Corregidor would, in due course, also fall to the enemy. It was being bombarded night and day.

"MacArthur was an American hero at the time. His capture by Japanese troops would have been unthinkable. For that reason, President Franklin Roosevelt finally ordered General MacArthur to evacuate Corregidor to a safer location, to Australia. Australia would be the springboard to start an American offensive in the Pacific."

"Yes, I recall the General departed on a patrol boat commanded by a Lieutenant Buckwheat or something like that," Freddy offers.

"You are correct again," Carmen replies. "However, patrol boat 41's skipper was Bulkeley, Lieutenant Bulkeley. He was also an American hero. And, just like the General, he received the highest military decoration possible, the Medal of Honor. He had a ship named after him in 2001, the *USS Bulkeley (DDG-84)*.

"At any rate, my ancestors arrived on Corregidor Island moments before the American's had finalized their escape plan. Within a few minutes of their arrival on the island, my ancestors quickly scurried across the mooring ropes onto Bulkeley's patrol boat. They hid near the bilges mere moments before the boat castoff in the dark.

"After leaving Corregidor, the boat, carrying the General, his family, and my stowaway ancestors traveled 560 miles to the Philippines island of Mindanao. A bit later my ancestors, hiding in a suitcase, boarded an aircraft that took them to northern Australia. The rest is history."

"Wow! So, your ancestors saw General MacArthur!" Freddy says. "That must have been totally awesome, totally cool!"

"Yes, Freddy, it certainly must have been," Carmen laughs. "And if you pause to consider it I bet my hungry ancestors ate a few meals with the General and his family as well! As you would expect, they were almost certainly hiding when they did so."

Freddy roars with delight as he visualizes Carmen's ancestors quietly sitting in the shadows. There they are, munching on crumbs stolen from PT-41's food stores.

"But, there is even more to the story, Freddy. My ancestors liked the MacArthur's, especially the General. So they hitched a ride in one of the General's staff officer's trunks and accompanied the General's staff everywhere that it went. General MacArthur eventually embarked onboard the *Nashville* like you said. My ancestors were pretty scared at first when they arrived on the ship. It was a huge ship in comparison to Lieutenant Bulkeley's patrol boat.

"It was very dangerous for mice aboard the ship. As you know, some badly behaved mice can be a real nuisance at times, gnawing on wood, eating holes in boxes of foodstuffs, things like that. It was that way aboard *Nashville*, misbehaving mice making a pest of themselves. So, like every other ship at the time, and even like today, the ship's mice were hunted down by the sailors. Traps were set and poisonous bait was liberally applied in many of the ship's compartments.

"Then again, some of the sailors did not consider mice as pests. Many of them kept a mouse or two as pets. There was one particular sailor on the ship, a Signalman First Class, who took all of my ancestors under his wing, sort of speaking. He went by the name of Jimbo. Jimbo was particularly fond of my Grandparents. He would lie in his rack - that's what they call a bed on a ship - and talk to my Grandparents. He usually did this after Taps so no one could hear him. Needless to say, Jimbo loved his pets.

"Well, on 13 December 1944, the *Nashville* was struck by a kamikaze plane off Negros Island in the southern part of the Philippines. It was during the Battle of Leyte Gulf as you mentioned. The kamikaze plane carried two bombs, both of which exploded about ten feet off of the ship's deck. One hundred thirty-three sailors were killed and one hundred ninety were wounded. One of those gravely wounded was the Signalman First Class, Jimbo."

Freddy ponders this.

Hmm, I wonder. My Grandfather was a signalman first class onboard *Nashville*. Could it have been him? Naw, no one in my family ever told me about talking mice. And I don't remember anyone referring to my Grandpa as Jimbo.

Carmen continues, saying, "My ancestors were devastated by the carnage on the ship. The aircraft had crashed into the ship's port five-inch gun mount which caused gasoline fires and ammunition to explode. The ship's midsection was a blazing inferno. It took days to extinguish the fires. Some of my ancestors and many of their friends perished in the fire. As you can well imagine since I am here with you, my Grandparents survived.

"General MacArthur had already departed *Nashville* before the ship was hit by the kamikaze plane. He had left the ship in October 1944 to establish his headquarters at Tacloban City. The city is on a large southern island called Leyte.

"My ancestors did not want to go ashore with the General's staff. The Mouse Purge was still fresh in their minds. So they stayed aboard *Nashville*. They unmistakably thought it was safer aboard the ship than being ashore. The kamikaze attack evidently changed their thoughts when it came to their wellbeing.

"The Attack Group Commander shifted his flag to *USS Dashiell* after the kamikaze attack on *Nashville*. That's when my Grandparents jumped ship sort of speaking as they hid once again in the trunk of a staff officer.

"Meanwhile, *Nashville* was temporarily out of the war. She steamed to the Puget Sound Naval Shipyard, arriving in mid-January 1945. She underwent extensive repairs. The ship didn't reenter the war until five months later, in May 1945.

"And this is where it gets really interesting, Freddy. My ancestors eventually jumped ship once again. It was during a replenishment at sea. They hid in a crate of peanuts of all things. After cross-decking, that's going from one ship to another, they eventually caught up once more with the General. They remained with his staff for the duration of the war.

"Now it's time for the coolest part, Freddy. As you probably know, as Supreme Commander, General MacArthur officiated over the formal surrender of Japanese troops onboard the battleship *USS Missouri* in Tokyo Harbor. My very own Grandfather was on the ship to witness the proceedings. If you look closely at pictures in history books, you can just about see him secretly watching the ceremony from behind the shoe of one of the officers standing behind the General!"

"You have got to be kidding!" Freddy exclaims. "So, your Grandfather was on the battleship *Missouri* when General MacArthur accepted Japan's unconditional surrender?"

"Yes, dear, he was," Carmen responds with a smile. "You see, Freddy my ancestors, were, at long last, living without fear of harassment for the first time in many years. They could not believe their good fortune. Regardless of the devastation that surrounded them they were living a life of comfort in the center of Tokyo. Many of my ancestors learned to speak Japanese. In fact, a few of them are in Japan today. They are performing on the stage. The Japanese simply adore them."

Carmen grins and says, "Long after the War, some of my ancestors hitched a ride as castaways on another warship that was returning to the Continental United States. After they had arrived, some of my ancestors went east, some went south, and some went north. As for my Grandparents, they found their permanent home in Los Angeles, California. That's where I was born."

With an enormous smile and an even larger sigh, Carmen says, "Well, there you have it. That is my story, Freddy."

As he stares at Carmen, Freddy's mind is racing.

Wow, I can only imagine if Grandpa was alive to hear this story. He would be thrilled! And, if the story wasn't told to me by a mouse, I bet Papa would think the story was just as grand as I think it is. But, why am I jabbering so? No one would believe I heard the story from a mouse on my very first day on the job at Lloyd's Pet Shoppe.

With an impulsive outburst that startles Carmen, Freddy shouts, "Oh my goodness! I have to clean up the Shoppe."

He glances at his watch and screams in horror, "And I have only an hour to do it!"

CHAPTER FOUR
FREDDY LOOK WHAT YOU DID!

Freddy is worried. He has been in Lloyd's Pet Shoppe what seems like forever, and he has not accomplished a single chore to clean up the store. His boss, Mister Lloyd, will arrive in exactly one hour! Instead of working, Freddy has been talking all the while to his reddish-brown mouse friend, Carmen. He's also been listening with fascination as Carmen told her amazing story about her heroic ancestors.

"Thank you, Carmen. That was a fantastic story," Freddy whispers. "But, please help me out here. We only have an hour to go before Mister Lloyd arrives. How are we going to prepare the Shoppe for his arrival?"

"Leave it to me," Carmen replies. "Unlock the cages of the other mice, including Brutus' cage. Then get me those items I need from Mister Lloyd's desk if you please. After that sit back, relax, and enjoy as you watch the leadership prowess of an American red-headed mouse in action!"

Freddy opens all of the mouse cages. What transpires next is utterly astounding. Carmen officiates over a quick meeting with the other brown mice. She gives them specific assignments. Some are instructed to clean cages. Others are ordered to give the puppies some time to exercise in the enclosed pen out back. A few are directed to clean reptile cages and to scoop litter out of cat cages. Two are directed to scrape poop off of the bird perches.

Except for the three Aussies, the remaining mice are instructed to feed and water the animals. Carmen gives the choicest assignment to Peter and Charlie. They are obliged to remove the dead goldfish from the aquariums, a task they accept with pleasure.

Brutus refuses to accept any tasks. He merely sits sulking in the middle of the floor tapping his cane and muttering to himself.

Freddy is pleased to see the mice are cleaning cages, sweeping the floor, clearing out dead goldfish, and giving all the puppies a chance to stretch their legs. Then he stealthily strides into Mister Lloyd's office. As he does, he makes a silent wish Mister Lloyd will not notice anything amiss on or in his desk.

After he obtains the items that Carmen had requested from Mister Lloyd's desk, Freddy returns to the Shoppe's main area. He breathes a sigh of relief. All is going perfectly well according to Carmen's well-thought out plan. There is no need for him to worry.

"Carmen," he says smiling, "here are the things you wanted. Hurry up, okay? I want to return these items to Mister Lloyd's desk before he arrives."

Carmen replies, "You got it, darling. I only need fifteen minutes or so to complete my project." She notices the satisfied look on Freddy's face. He is obviously pleased with the cleanup activity in the store. She adds, "Now do you trust me, Freddy?"

"Of course I do," Freddy replies with a big smile. "However, I feel a little guilty. You mice are doing all of my chores, and I'm going to get all of the credit. It just doesn't seem fair, if you know what I mean."

"Oh, don't worry yourself over such a trivial matter," Carmen replies with a good-natured laugh. "You will be able to pay us back soon enough."

Freddy's look is one of misunderstanding.

What did she say? Did she just say something about my being able to pay them back soon enough? What does she mean by that? Before he can ask, he notices Carmen is staring at him, her eyes searching his own.

Goodness! Carmen is talking to me and I'm not paying attention!

"I'm sorry, Carmen," he stammers. "Did you say something?"

"I said I am famished, darling. Could you please get me a handful of mice pellets from the storeroom? My feeding tray is empty, has been for a day now. While you are in there, you should get yourself a frosty Coca-Cola out of the fridge. All this dust in the store can make you thirsty."

Then, with a serious look on her face, she says, "And while you're at it, you better straighten the storeroom as well. Mister Lloyd can be pretty bad-tempered when it comes to the storeroom. He likes it neat and tidy. Just bring my feed along when you're finished doing what you must in the storeroom, okay?"

"Okay, and yes I am thirsty now that you mention it," Freddy replies with a smile. He pulls his Composition notebook out of his pocket and looks at page three. Written in bold letters in his handwriting are the words, *Do not forget to straighten the storeroom!*

"Thanks for reminding me about straightening the storeroom. I almost forgot about that. I'll get you some feed, too. I will be back in a jiffy."

Freddy glimpses at his watch. It is five minutes after nine. Mister Lloyd will arrive in exactly twenty-five minutes.

At the rate the mice are working, all my chores will be completed on time. Then all I will have to do is maintain the status quo for the rest of the work day. What could be easier?

Freddy takes his time straightening the storeroom. He also takes a good look around. This is the first opportunity he has had to peer into containers, boxes, and other supplies for the Pet Shoppe's animals. While he's busily straightening things and being nosy, he consults his watch from time to time.

After eighteen minutes or so in the storeroom, he grabs a Coke from the refrigerator. He pops it open and takes a huge gulp of the bottle's refreshingly fizzy brown liquid. He scoops a handful of mice pellets from the open grain sack. He suddenly feels hungry, but lunch is only a couple of hours away. He can wait.

Well, time to get back to work. Work - what a joke!

When Freddy reenters the Shoppe's sales floor, he is flabbergasted. He has to lean against the counter to keep from passing out. Every animal in the Shoppe, other than fish nonchalantly swimming in their aquariums, is gone!

But how did they disappear? Why? The Shoppe is swept clean, stinky poop is gone, and every cage is spic and span. But where are the animals? And where is Carmen?

Freddy exclaims aloud, "To think I trusted her! She complimented me over and over. She looked fondly into my eyes. She told me that story about General MacArthur and the nice sailor onboard *Nashville*. She told stories about talking brown mice and their dangerous exploits. She just wanted to soften me up, to keep me off balance. So she could escape. What a fool I am!"

At this very moment, Mister Lloyd stumbles into the Shoppe through the wide open front door. He does not need to look around. He knows. And he is fuming mad.

He yells, "Freddy, what have you done? All of my animals have escaped. Freddy! What have you done with my animals?"

He growls one last time, "Freddy, look what you did!"

Mister Lloyd never receives an answer from his assistant. That's because Freddy is racing like a wild stallion across the parking lot to the sanctuary of no place in particular. He does not care where he is headed. All he wants is to be as far away from Lloyd's Pet Shoppe as possible.

Finally, after a half-hour of sprinting across town and satisfied he is far enough away from the nightmare that just happened, Freddy stops. He is panting, trying to catch his breath. He sits down to rest against a tree. In a few minutes, he is fast asleep.

CHAPTER FIVE
MOUSE IN A SHOEBOX

It is much later in the evening when Freddy glances at his watch. He is still sitting in his bedroom, sent here hours ago by his Papa. The time is nine o'clock in the evening on what Freddy fears is going to be the darkest, most dreadful day of his young life.

He can still hear the muffled voices of his parents in the downstairs kitchen. They are having an animated conversation with Mister Lloyd. From what Freddy can recognize, his future does not look too promising.

Freddy cannot remember a more depressing, chaotic day. There was the one exception. It was the time his little sister, Betsy, got her big toe stuck in the tub's faucet while she was taking a bubble bath. She was six at the time. The plumbers had to tear out the whole wall behind the tub so they could get to the faucet.

Then they poured soapy water in the faucet to liberate her big toe. All the while Betsy was shattering everyone's ears with her screams as if there was no tomorrow.

From what he is able to glean from his parents' long-winded, three-hour conversation with Mister Lloyd, he is most likely without a summer job. There are also telltale overtones creeping up the stairs about monetary reparations having to be paid to Mister Lloyd for lost revenue. Eventually, the muffled voices in the kitchen lower to a normal decibel. Thanks are exchanged and a good-bye is spoken. It is answered by "Have a great night, Mister Lloyd. Thanks again!"

Mister Lloyd is leaving! Thank goodness. Oh, but what is going to happen to me? Mama and Papa are going to be furious!

Are those footsteps on the stairs? Oh no! Papa is coming up the stairs! The hour of reckoning nears! Someone is knocking on my bedroom door! It's Papa! Say goodbye to the cruel world, Freddy, because you're a goner!

"Freddy, unlock your door. We need to talk."

"Yes, sir, I'll unlock it right away sir!"

"Sit down, young man," his Papa orders as he enters Freddy's room. "Let us get one thing straight right up front. What you supposedly did today was totally out of character for you. I know you, son. I know you all too well. There was no way you would have allowed all of those animals to escape from their cages. I do not doubt your honesty, trustworthiness, and integrity at all. I want you to know that before we discuss anything else."

"Thank you, sir," Freddy responds with a meek smile.

Whew! This is going better than I planned. Maybe this will not be as tough as I thought it would be. I expected Papa to be a lot angrier.

"Freddy, Mister Lloyd and the other store managers on the block located most of the animals. That's very fortunate for you."

Freddy smiles timidly.

Yes! Most of the animals have been returned to the store. My allowance and meager piggy bank savings may survive this disaster after all. Moreover, I am happy and relieved that most of the animals have been returned.

"Freddy, I suspect you are relieved that most of the animals have been found. However, I would not get too smiley too soon if I were you. There are a couple of other serious items that still remain."

Freddy's feeble smile vanishes in a flash.

Oh, no. No, no, no! Mister Lloyd discovered I stole from his desk! Papa always said there is nothing crummier than a thief. Yes, I'll think it again. Goodbye cruel world, because Freddy is about to depart, forever! Thanks a bunch, Carmen. Thanks for nothing!

"You see, Freddy, despite their best efforts, Mister Lloyd and the other town square's shop owners did not find a single, solitary brown mouse in the Shoppe. Nor were there any brown mice within a twenty-foot radius of the building or even on the adjacent lot.

They found every other animal, to include all of the white mice. But they could not find a single brown mouse!"

Freddy is frantic, his mind racing a gazillion miles a second.

Oh no! Not the talking mice. What could have happened to Carmen, the three talking Aussies, and the other members of the famous dance troupe? What have I done?

"Freddy," his Papa continues, "you may or may not know this, but Mister Lloyd's brown mice were valuable. There was also a very rare reddish-brown female mouse with quite unusual looking red hair on the top of her head. According to Mister Lloyd, she is priceless and irreplaceable."

Freddy is staring at the floor. His face is one of shock. His mind is almost numb as he thinks about Carmen. Papa, if only you knew the truth how priceless Carmen is!

Freddy's Papa says, "Mister Lloyd purchased his brown mice from an Australian businessman who, for some reason, wishes to remain anonymous. As I just said, the redheaded female mouse was especially priceless. In fact, she is a one-of-a-kind mouse. As I said, she is irreplaceable." He grins.

"And Freddy, unlike the white mice, all of the brown mice in Mister Lloyd's Pet Shoppe were pedigrees. That means they were pure blooded mice, quite valuable to say the least. Do you know what I mean by the word pedigree?"

Freddy nods his head in agreement as his thoughts go wild. He lowers his head and closes his eyes.

Certainly, I know what a pedigree is. Is that the only concern here, pedigrees? No, there is more, much more. If only you knew Papa! These mice talked to me. Carmen and the brown mice have ancestors who knew General MacArthur, an American icon. The brown mice's ancestors survived World War II in the Philippines. They escaped Corregidor Island along with General MacArthur and his family on Lieutenant Bulkeley's patrol boat.

Then they went to Australia. From there, they went to the *USS Nashville* then crossed-decked many ships until they ended up in Japan. Carmen's Grandfather actually attended the ceremony on *USS Missouri* that ended World War II in the Pacific!

Finally, Carmen's Grandparents moved to Los Angeles. Carmen and the three Aussies are direct descendants of heroes! And Papa, these mice can talk. They know how to dance, to sing, to entertain. So, what is all this ridiculous talk about mere pedigrees? There is more, much more to the story!

Freddy looks up at his Papa and stares.

"There is something else, son."

Oh no! Here's the kicker. Here comes the desk caper lecture, I know it! I'm a goner for sure! I stole from Mister Lloyd and they know!

"Someone will have to pay Mister Lloyd a portion of the money he lost as a result of his store closing for a few hours while he searched for his missing animals."

There go my allowance and my summer vacation! I'll be doing odd jobs around the neighborhood all summer just to pay back Mister Lloyd!

"He estimates he lost at least three hundred dollars in sales."

I owe him three hundred dollars? How am I ever going to get that kind of money? I could work odd jobs every summer until I'm in college and never earn that much money!

"However, Mister Lloyd is an agreeable man. He told me he vividly remembers his first job as a kid. He said he made plenty of mistakes. He was surprised he did not get fired after the first week. He and I have settled on an agreement that should be to everyone's liking."

Mister Lloyd made mistakes? No way! As far as his being an agreeable man, well, you do not want my opinion on that, Papa! He also has a thing about pet poop. Ugh!

"There is also the issue of compensating Mister Lloyd for the nineteen brown mice and the reddish-brown female mouse. They seem to have vanished into thin air. Since they were pedigrees, Mr. Lloyd estimates it will cost five dollars apiece to replace nineteen of them."

Freddy's Papa says with a big grin, "As I said a minute ago, the female is irreplaceable; at least that is what I was led to believe by Mister Lloyd. Yes, she is a one-of-a-kind, rare mouse." He grins again. "There is no other mouse like her in the world."

Huh? Hey, Papa, why do you grin every time you mention the priceless redheaded female mouse? Is there something I'm missing here?

"The way I figure it, Freddy," his Papa continues in a serious manner, "you owe Mister Lloyd ninety-five dollars for the nineteen missing brown mice." He grins again, saying, "As far as the missing redheaded mouse is concerned, I took care of that in a different way." The grin on Papa's face is unmistakable once more.

Only ninety-five dollars! For mice that can talk? Ninety-five dollars and for offspring of war heroes no less! I owe less than one hundred measly dollars for descendants of mice that witnessed the Bataan Death March? Ninety-five dollars for nineteen heroic mice whose ancestors experienced the Mouse Purge, underwent bombings at Corregidor, escaped from the Philippines along with General MacArthur? And Carmen, how can anyone put a price tag on her? How?

But what's this? Papa is grinning once again. Moreover, he said he took care of reimbursing Mister Lloyd for Carmen in a different way. What does that mean? Did he pay an extraordinary restitution to Mister Lloyd for Carmen?

"Freddy, after a long and very heated discussion with Mister Lloyd, Mama and I have decided to agree to Mister Lloyd's demands."

Ouch! The moment has arrived at last. I am doomed beyond recognition. I will be giving my allowance to Mister Lloyd until I am eighteen years old and probably far beyond that!

"Starting tomorrow, you will report to Lloyd's Pet Shoppe where you will work for full wages. Obviously, you will be on probation, but that is understandable given the circumstances. When you get paid each Friday, you will hand over five dollars of your wages to Mister Lloyd.

"After you have paid him the grand total of twenty-five dollars, your debt to him will be forgiven. You are a lucky fellow, Freddy. Mister Lloyd could have fired you. Additionally, he could have demanded over three hundred dollars restitution for lost revenue and ninety-five dollars to replace his missing brown mice." He grins again, adding, "And of course, there is the issue of paying him even more money for the red-headed mouse."

Freddy once again sees that his Papa is grinning after he makes mention of Carmen.

"Yet, he knows you are an honest boy who does not steal like some other boys your age." This causes Freddy's stomach to tighten.

"He also realizes you are worth every cent of your wages. You are a hard worker. In fact, Mister Lloyd cannot recall a time when an assistant completed chores as quickly and diligently as you did this morning. He had said, other than the missing animals, of course, the Shoppe was the cleanest he had ever seen it in all his years as its owner."

Twenty-five dollars and my debts are forgiven? This is great! I will still have over fifty dollars spending money each week. Best of all, I will keep my summer job. Maybe Mister Lloyd will let me work part-time in his store when school is back in session! Wow! Mister Lloyd is really a swell guy after all. So are you, Papa.

"Now, Freddy," his Father continues, "Do you understand everything I just told you?"

"Yes, sir, I sure do. Thanks for sticking up for me. It really means a lot to me, Papa. You're the greatest father a guy could have."

His Papa smiles saying, "You are welcome, son. I have total confidence in your ability to make things right. However, there is one final matter that needs to be addressed."

No! Not the desk incident! Why would Mister Lloyd want me back, knowing I snuck into his office and took something from his desk? That I stole from him? Violated his trust?

Now his Papa has a mischievous smile on his face.

Freddy's Papa says, "There remains the matter of how so many animals could simply walk out of their cages. All the while you were busily making Lloyd's Pet Shoppe look better than it ever has since the store has opened. There is also the issue of how twenty valuable brown mice, which includes the rare redheaded female, could vanish without a trace. If I did not know better, I would suspect that somebody, perhaps *something*, was behind the escape caper."

He continues to stare at Freddy. "You simply could not have accomplished so many things at once. You may be speedy, but I know you too well, son. You have a tendency to procrastinate. However, someday you will know who, in fact, released all the animals because both of us know it was not you who did so.

"You see son," his father whispers with a broad smile on his face, "I once had a shoe box with a brown mouse in it. I kept it hidden in my closet. It was a special mouse, Freddy, a really special mouse. Someday when it's not too late at night as it is now, I will tell you all about it." He glances at Freddy's wristwatch.

"But, it is nearly nine-thirty. You need to get ready for bed fairly soon. Tomorrow's another day. Good-night son. Count your blessings, because you really lucked out this time, young man!"

"Goodnight, Papa," Freddy replies with a smile. "And thanks again."

What in the world was that all about? What was Papa hinting at when he mentioned an escape caper? I never knew Papa had a box with a brown mouse in it when he was a kid. What did he mean when he said that his mouse was special? I wonder.

As he goes into the bathroom to brush his teeth, Freddy suddenly realizes he is exhausted. It has been a tough, grueling day full of emotion and far too much excitement. However, he is very happy. Everything had turned out okay after all.

He is forgiven by Mister Lloyd and by his parents. He still has his new job. He will have money to spend all summer long on goodies and fun things. He also had made a good impression on Mister Lloyd, thanks to Carmen and nineteen extremely talented brown mice.

Returning to his bedroom, Freddy sits in his bed and thinks about what transpired at Lloyd's Pet Shoppe. Despite his somewhat happy and relieved mood, Freddy begins to feel miserable. He already misses Carmen and the others. Then he shakes his head a few times.

No. What I saw and heard, in reality, was probably nothing more than a figment of my imagination. There are no special brown mice. No way! Maybe I fell asleep after I completed my chores. Then I some-how left the cages and pens open. Yes! That is what happened. I must have fallen asleep, and somehow the animals escaped out of the front door. I must have been dreaming about everything else the entire time.

Nope! There is no Carmen. There are no talking Aussie mice. There is no dance troupe. There are no mouse heroes. There was no adventurous escape from the Philippines, at least as it concerned mice. It was my imagination playing tricks on me once again.

CHAPTER SIX
HE'S THE LINCHPIN!

Freddy is just about to turn off his bedroom light. It has been a very busy, exciting, but rather confusing day for him. He somehow allowed all the animals to escape from Lloyd's Pet Shoppe. All were recovered except for nineteen brown mice and one reddish-brown mouse. They were never found. Happily, all he has to do is pay Mister Lloyd twenty-five dollars in restitution. Miraculously, he has retained his job.

What is more miraculous, Freddy figures he must have imagined having a conversation with four mice at the Shoppe. He had also imagined listening to an exciting story told by a lovable, reddish-brown, redheaded mouse named Carmen.

Yes, I must have imagined it. Mice can't talk. There's no mouse troupe. And there's no Carmen.

Plus the story about the nice sailor on *Nashville* never happened at least as it concerned mice.

Oh well, so much for one more exciting day of make-believe as my imagination once again ran away with my mind. It's time to turn off the light and get some sleep. Tomorrow is another day, another fun-filled day at Lloyd's Pet Shoppe and day long cleaning of poop.

Suddenly, harmonious ragtime music in an eerily hushed manner fills the room.

What is this, music - singing? It appears to be coming from under the bed! Could it be? No, there is no way Carmen and the Aussies could be in this room.

Stop it Freddy! Get a grip. You've had a nightmarish day. There are no special, talking mice. There are no descendants of heroes in this room. Yet! You *are* still awake. So are *not* dreaming. The singing *is* real, and it's coming from beneath your bed!

As if to confirm his subconscious suspicions, a horde of nineteen furry brown mice crawls up the comforter to appear at the foot of Freddy's bed.

Freddy instantly recognizes the first of three mice as they saunter over to him one by one from the end of the bed.

"Hey, mate!"

It's the Aussie, Peter!

"Thanks for giving us the opportunity to escape, Freddy. We couldn't have done it without you, Freddy, ole pal! And to think I mistrusted you. Mate, I was so wrong."

"Hello there, you noble, large human," says another mouse.

It's the terrorizing Aussie mouse, Brutus!

"I didn't think you had it in you, Freddy. When Carmen and I talked about you last night, I was opposed to the idea. I never thought you would open up all the cages. But you did. Then you purposely turned your back for a few minutes to grab a Coca-Cola in the back room so we could escape. Carmen told us all about it. You sure had me fooled. I owe you an apology." He taps his cane on Freddy's foot and exclaims, "I'm sorry I doubted you. I thank you, mate!"

"Hello, Freddy! Have you gutted anyone with your Swiss pocketknife yet?"

It's the third Aussie, Charlie!

"Carmen was certain Mister Lloyd would eventually come to your house to speak to your parents. So she ordered the troupe to hide out in the back seat of Mister Lloyd's car. We got here by hitching a free ride." He laughs.

"Mister Lloyd had angrily thrown his baloney and cheese sandwich onto the back seat." He rubs his fat belly. "We even had a delicious snack on the way, Cheetoes too." He giggles.

"And to think we didn't believe you could pull it off, Freddy. But you did. You even retained your job. I hope you aren't sore with us."

Freddy's mind is racing at the speed of sound.

Sore? What do you mean, sore? Of course, I'm sore, Charlie. You mice almost cost me my job, my reputation, my life's allowance, and my entire existence as a happy, well-adjusted teenager! But, everything turned out okay, didn't it? You gave the

Shoppe a spic and span shine to impress Mister Lloyd. And I got all of the credit. So, as the saying goes, I guess all is well that ends well.

"No, Charlie, I'm not sore at you or any of the others," Freddy responds, "at least not anymore. However, please tell me why you had to use me to escape."

"I think I can answer that, darling."

Carmen! Carmen is wearing a lovely, tight-fitting blue gown with tiny silver sequins.

So that is why she wanted me to get the needle and thread from Mister Lloyd's desk. She wanted to put the finishing touches on her new gown. Golly, she looks beautiful!

"I am very sorry, darling," Carmen softly whispers as she casually strides onto Freddy's lap. She sits down on her haunches.

Looking up at him she says, "On the surface, I guess it appears that we, or perhaps I should say that I used you. In reality, Freddy, perhaps I did. However, I never intended for my plan to be wicked. Please trust me when I say that.

"You see, Freddy, Mister Lloyd never intended to keep us for one moment longer than necessary for him to turn a hefty profit. He knew we were valuable mice. He is an experienced handler of mice and other exotic animals. He suspected the brown mice were extraordinary.

"Plus, he somehow knew we could talk. Despite his repeated attempts to get us to talk, I'm happy to say we never swallowed the bait." She laughs, and then she whispers, "I dare say, each of us remained as silent as a mouse."

Then, with a sad look, Carmen says with a sigh, "When all is said and done, it would appear the greediness of instant, high profits speaks louder than conscience. So it was with Mister Lloyd. This past Wednesday he sold the others to the highest bidder." She appears to recoil as she says this. Tears begin to well in her eyes.

"The highest bidder was a regional Cub Scout director. The director was going to return to the store to pick up the others at eleven o'clock this very morning! He told Mister Lloyd he intended to auction them off one by one during a regional Cub Scout fundraising Jamboree this weekend."

With an annoyed sneer, she adds, "As for me, Mister Lloyd had been calling pet shops around the country to sell me to the highest bidder as well. Apparently I am worth more than one hundred dollars, probably because of my red hair." She shrugs her shoulders and bats her eyelids at least five times.

"Just like the human population, where roughly two percent of the world's population is naturally redheaded, as a redheaded mouse, I am just as rare. With my blue eyes, it would appear I'm even rarer."

Carmen tilts her head to one side, shrugs her shoulders, and bats her eyelids a few more times. Then she combs her redheaded locks with her claws. She's clearly showing off her good looks.

"Freddy, could you imagine our sorrow if the others were taken into captivity in nineteen separate homes, never to see each other again? Can you imagine how sad it would be if they were given away to some three-ring circus or worse? Parents, children, spouses, and friends of us mice would be stripped of their family ties forever. All of us would have been devastated.

"More importantly, the troupe would never again perform for grateful audiences. Then I would have been taken to goodness knows where to be displayed as someone's trophy." She closes her eyes and shivers.

"So you see, my dear, Freddy, we simply had to escape from Lloyd's Pet Shoppe. And we had to escape before Mister Lloyd's arrival at the pet store at nine-thirty this morning. I hope you understand. I hope you are not angry with me. More importantly, I hope you can forgive me."

"Aw, I am not angry, Carmen, especially not with you," Freddy says. "I could never get angry with you. Plus there is nothing to forgive. I guess I am a bit confused, that's all. So many remarkable things have happened today. I simply do not understand all of it."

"No one could expect that you should understand it all, darling. So, let me give it to you straight, okay?

"The three Aussies are making preparations for the troupe to leave early tomorrow morning on a Greyhound bus bound for New York City. A special friend of ours is going to smuggle the troupe onto the bus." She winks at Charlie.

"We heard there are hundreds of special brown mice in New York City living in a community of artists, musicians, and performers. With a little bit of luck, our troupe will be able to join them." She laughs loudly exclaiming, "Broadway, here we come!"

"Tell me it's not true, Carmen!" Freddy gasps. "You're going to leave? We just met this very morning!"

"No, darling, not all of us are leaving. Only nineteen mice are leaving. One will be staying." She smiles playfully.

Freddy turns his head from Carmen. He doesn't want her to see the tears of sadness in his eyes. He shudders.

One mouse is staying? It's probably Brutus. Brutus is old and feeble. He needs a cane to walk. But it doesn't matter. He will be taken care of; I'll make sure of it. After all, he may be crabby, but the Aussie is getting on in years.

With his head still turned away from Carmen, Freddy asks in a whisper, "Which one of you is going to stay, Carmen?"

Carmen surprises Freddy as she jumps up and down on his lap. She yells, "I am! I am the one who is going to stay behind, Freddy! Isn't that awesome?"

Freddy turns to look at her. Despite tears flowing down his cheek, he is sporting a huge smile. He quickly wipes away the tears with the back of his hand.

He thinks about this for a moment. Then he says excitedly, "I am thrilled Carmen! You are attractive, smart, and daring. More importantly, you're really a first-rate friend. Knowing you are going to stay behind is wonderful news. And to think I thought boring, lazy, obnoxious Brutus was going to stay behind!"

Freddy quickly turns to look at Brutus. Brutus is sitting beside him on the bed. He says, "Sorry, mate, I didn't mean anything spiteful by that."

Brutus simply smiles and nods his head.

Turning his attention back to Carmen, Freddy says with a whisper, "That's totally wonderful, Carmen. But why are *you* staying behind? Why are you not going to New York City with the rest of your troupe?"

"Oh, Freddy, I am an old fashioned gal. Like most strong-willed American females, I am very independent. As you know, I never was a very good troupe member. I cannot act or sing. And you know I cannot dance." She laughs with embarrassment.

"I simply handle the troupe's paperwork. Besides, the others knew I would eventually leave their company. I only started to hang around the troupe when I learned Miser Lloyd was planning to buy the mice from the anonymous Australian businessman.

"You see, Freddy, I was on vacation in Australia visiting relatives when I learned about Mister Lloyd's purchase. I was incredibly excited as you can well imagine. I would finally be able to hitch a ride and come here to Buffalo. My Mother lived a good portion of her adult life in this city. She had moved here from Los Angeles after my Daddy died. So I had heard many terrific stories about the city and its people."

Her eyes squint as she tilts her head to the left. She says, "So I managed to make a few phone calls as I finalized my devious plan."

With a grin, she adds, "I also sort of knew the anonymous Australian businessman of which your Papa mentioned. Anyway, Mister Lloyd's purchase of the nineteen brown mice seemed like my free, one-way ticket to happiness. So I hopped on board, smuggling in a suitcase of all places." She frowns.

"In spite of my jubilation with finally being in Buffalo, Mister Lloyd went and sold the others to an auctioneer before I could make arrangements to get us out of the Pet Shoppe. Fortunately, everything worked out well in the end, yes?"

"Yes, it did, and I am thrilled you will be staying behind, Carmen. But, where are you going to live? What are you going to do?"

"Well, if it is not too much trouble, I would like to live here. Maybe I can live in your shoe, perhaps in your discarded lunch box, or in the back of your closet." She frowns.

"But no, your closet is dreadfully messy so it will not do at all. I am no trouble, Freddy, I can assure you. Besides, your parents will not mind, especially Papa."

Freddy looks surprised. My parents won't mind, especially Papa. How is that?

"What do you mean my Papa will not mind, Carmen?"

"Oh, that is right, darling. I almost forgot your Papa did not tell you his story about the mouse that he hid in his shoebox as a young boy, did he?"

"No, Carmen, he did not. He said he would tell me someday when it isn't so late at night as it is right now." He glances at his watch.

"Well, there is no harm in my NOT telling you then either, is there, darling?"

Freddy's mind is racing.

How do you know about that story, Carmen? How could you possibly know about the story my Papa has yet to tell me?

Freddy sighs and says, "I guess not, Carmen. I guess I can wait."

With his face noticeably flushed, he says in a soft voice, "And yes, Carmen, I would love for you to live here. It makes me very happy knowing you want to live with me."

Carmen folds her front legs across her chest in a show of female tenacity. "Okay then, it is settled. I shall live here, in your discarded lunch box unless, of course, you have a decent shoebox." She giggles. "But, I must warn you, I like a clean, organized, and tidy room."

She slowly shakes her head as she glances around Freddy's messy room. "I must also say I despise shredded newspapers. I prefer cotton bedding. I deserve the best. After all, you *will* be living with a star, yes?"

"Cool and yes and okay, sounds awesome. But, tell me, Carmen, why do you want to live here of all places?"

"Three reasons, Freddy. One, don't you believe for a moment that Mister Lloyd was as forgiving as you think. Please do not tell anybody, but your Papa gave Mister Lloyd four hundred dollars to forget the whole incident and to allow you to continue working at the store. That was a whopping one hundred dollars more than Mister Lloyd's estimate of lost revenue which, in my opinion, was grossly inflated.

"I dare say Mister Lloyd disagreed at first. But he finally conceded when he saw four one hundred dollar bills your Papa had placed on the kitchen table."

"Wow! My Papa did that for me?"

"Yes, Freddy, he sure did. Your Papa loves you a lot. And why shouldn't he? You are a great kid, Freddy. Quite handsome too, I might add." She giggles as Freddy blushes once more.

"That brings me to reason number two. Why in the world did you think I made this gown?"

Freddy shrugs.

"I made it for you, Freddy. Do you want to know why?"

Freddy's face turns a bit redder. "You really made that gown for me? It's very pretty, Carmen. And yes, of course, I want to know why."

"I made the gown because I love you. I have loved you as only a true friend could love another friend the very moment I laid my eyes on you. I have known everything about you for many years. In a way, Freddy, it is almost as though we have been acquainted with each other all of our lives. It is if we are brother and sister, long lost siblings getting acquainted for the first time. The only difference is you are a teenage boy and I am a girl mouse."

I feel the same way. Wait! She has known everything about me for years? Ah ha! Now I remember where I saw that medallion before I met Carmen. I saw it in a picture. Papa has an old black and white picture of Grandpa in his photo album. Grandpa is holding a brown mouse in his palm. The mouse is wearing a medallion that looks exactly like the one Carmen has around her neck!

"I am sorry to get off of the subject again, Carmen," Freddy asks. But I have a question. Does that medallion you are wearing have anything to do with my Grandfather?"

Carmen smiles deviously as she lifts the medallion to look at it. She avoids his eyes, saying, "Oh, I do believe it does, Freddy. It is a present handed down by my Grandmother. She got it from Jimbo on *USS Nashville*. Jimbo had given it to my Grandmother moments before my Grandparents left the ship."

Now it is Carmen's turn to blush. She says, "It would appear my Grandmother was Jimbo's favorite mouse. My Grandmother gave this medallion to my

Mother. Then my Mother gave it to me, and now I wear it proudly each and every day."

As she continues to look at the medallion, still avoiding Freddy's questioning eyes, she says, "This medallion is a minuscule Purple Heart. It is a reproduction of the one awarded to Jimbo in recognition of his being wounded in action. It is awarded in the name of the President of the United States. It contains a profile of General George Washington, our great nation's first President."

She holds the medallion in front of her. "Look, Freddy. Read the words on the reverse."

Freddy tries to read the words inscribed on the back of the medallion, but the writing is too small. "I can't," he says. "The writing is too tiny. Will you read it to me, please?"

"Of course I will, darling. It says in bold, capitalized letters, 'For Military Merit.' The reverse side also has a raised bronze heart below the coat of arms and leaves.'"

"Wow!" Freddy exclaims. "Let me see if I understand you correctly. The Signalman First Class, Jimbo, gave your Grandmother a reproduction of his Purple Heart. Your Grandmother gave it to your Mother, who gave it to you. That's totally awesome!"

Freddy scratches his head in thought.

That explains the picture of Grandpa holding a mouse that's wearing a medallion. And Grandpa was stationed on the ship that served as the flagship for General Douglas MacArthur, during the Allied invasion of Leyte Gulf in the Philippine Sea - *USS Nashville*. Plus he was a Signalman First Class!

And there's more! Grandpa was wounded during the kamikaze attack! He received a Purple Heart. That's the connection! Grandpa must have somehow known Carmen's Grandparents!

Grandpa is the Signalman First Class, the sailor that talked to mice as he lay on his rack, the one they called Jimbo! Furthermore - now I remember! Grandpa's closest friends would sometimes call him Jimbo! Jimbo and Grandpa are one in the same. Jimbo is

Grandpa and Grandpa is Jimbo, the Signalman First Class! My Grandpa Jimbo knew Carmen's Grandparents! This is totally out of this world super awesome!

Freddy finally realizes that Carmen has been staring at him intently while he was deep in thought. He also sees she has that all-too-familiar devious smirk on her face. He watches in confusion as her smirk slowly transforms into a wide grin. She abruptly looks away to avoid his eyes.

"Okay, love," she says as she bends down to smooth her gown. She avoids Freddy's eyes while she speaks. "Now that you know the connection between my Grandparents and Jimbo onboard *Nashville*, what do you say we get back to the topic at hand? Let us return to the remaining reason why I wish to stay here with you, okay?"

"Sure," Freddy replies with a big grin, "Go ahead, Carmen."

"Here is reason number three. I was told by a nameless person you have been having difficulty with math for a couple of years running, to include attending summer school on two occasions. Am I correct in my assumption?"

Freddy nods his head. He avoids Carmen's eyes. He's embarrassed. He gets A's and B's in every subject, even social studies, by oh! He surely struggles with math.

He says softly, "You bet I have. But how do you know? Who could have told you?"

Carmen ignores his questions, saying, "Freddy, darling, did you not know I have a doctorate in education from UCLA like my Mother? And guess what? My most favorite subject is math! I got all A's in all of my math classes throughout high school - Algebra, Geometry, Trigonometry, Calculus, you get the picture."

Freddy grins. Then his eyes open wide with recognition. Wait a minute here! Papa went to UCLA! Papa and Carmen's Mother probably knew each other in college! Does Papa know the real story about the mice in Mister Lloyd's store? I bet he does! That would explain why he was not upset about the brown mice that went missing. Oh, Papa, you are a sly one!

Could it be true? Could it have been that Carmen's Mother was the special mouse that used to hide in Papa's shoe box? Did Carmen's Mother know me, maybe when I was a baby? If so, that would explain why Carmen also knows me. Her Mother must have told her all about me!

Papa! He's the reason I got the job at Lloyd's Pet Shoppe. And the anonymous businessman from Australia - I bet Papa had something to do with that as well. He's definitely the anonymous, pretend Australian businessman. Papa just returned from a business trip to Australia. Yes, that's the link!

Carmen said she was visiting relatives in Australia before she hitched a ride with the rest of the troupe. I believe Papa orchestrated the entire thing, with Carmen's help of course. That would also explain the escape caper from Lloyd's Pet's Shoppe. Papa somehow found out Mister Lloyd had sold his special brown mice to an auctioneer. Then he also must have known Mister Lloyd was looking to sell Carmen to the highest bidder. I bet Carmen told him!

Finally, Papa pays Mister Lloyd four hundred dollars this evening to forget everything, to make the whole thing disappear very quietly. Evidently, he pretended he had no idea how special the brown mice really were!

The escape from Lloyd's Pet Shoppe was certainly coordinated as well. Carmen was working on the inside with Papa's help from the outside. I'm sure of it! Allowing all of the animals to get away was most likely a distraction so the brown mice could flee for good.

I bet Papa opened some of the cages himself while I was in the storage room. And there I was, straightening around, being nosy, and drinking a Coke and getting feed for Carmen; oblivious to what was happening in the Shoppe. While I was distracted in the storeroom, the animals in Lloyd's Pet Shoppe were being set free!

Yes, it all makes sense now. No wonder Carmen said she knows everything about me and my family.

Our families have been friends for generations, at least since my Grandpa's days on board *Nashville!* As Carmen said, she and I are practically related! And my wonderful Papa orchestrated the entire caper at Lloyd's Pet Shoppe, from beginning to end.

It's Papa! He's the linchpin!

Carmen is intently watching Freddy the entire time he is deep in thought. She finally breaks into his thoughts, stating, "Yes, I can see it now, you and me, Freddy, attending class together. I will be in your pocket as you go to school and no one will ever know."

She smiles. "We will eat lunch together. We will ride your bicycle together. We will go hiking and camping together. We will roller skate together. We will go to church together. And we will giggle when you eat fast food because no one will know I am there!"

With a huge grin she adds, "And just so you know, I love French fries dipped in honey mustard sauce! Plus, my favorite coffee in the morning is hazelnut." She laughs and Freddy laughs as well.

"We will do everything together, and you and I will never be lonely for each other's friendship. We will have a blast, Freddy! You can bet your bottom dollar we will. And you will get straight A's because I will help you with your math homework every night."

Out of the blue, Freddy scoops Carmen's petite, furry body into the palm of his hand. Then he gently closes his fingers around her in a loving embrace. He places his hand with Carmen in it against his chest. Tears of happiness are falling from his eyes. He now has the special friend of which he has always dreamed.

Carmen feels Freddy's rapidly heart beating next to hers. She also senses the sincere love radiating from Freddy's tender embrace. She giggles uncontrollably. Tears of happiness begin to flow down her furry cheeks.

He knows! We both know! We are going to be together forever!

(Continue reading - there's more to this story in the Epilogue.)

EPILOGUE

Many years later, when Freddy was very much older and his hair was turning gray, he told his grandchildren all about Carmen and her dance troupe. Freddy's four grandchildren, Micah, Julian, Gianna, and Joy listened attentively, their eyes wide with wonder.

Stories about talking animals never cease to amaze youngsters. I've also known plenty of teenagers and even a quantity of adults who occasionally enjoy reading an exciting story about talking animals. These kinds of stories let us escape reality, to visit a make-believe world where we secretly long to go every now and then. In all honesty, and in spite of everything, some of us truly never grow up. I know I haven't. Perhaps you haven't as well. Being young and free is breathtaking! Wouldn't you agree?

Carmen lived with Freddy for more than three decades. After Freddy was married, Carmen would sit at the dinner table along with Freddy and his wife. The three of them would have the most attention-grabbing conversations. Carmen would delight Freddy's wife with her tall tales of mouse adventures. Of course, Freddy never tired of hearing Carmen tell stories about Jimbo, the *Nashville*, and the many heroic exploits by Carmen's ancestors.

The three of them went on trips together, just husband and wife and Freddy's best friend, Carmen. Because it was easier to bring along a mouse in such a manner, most trips were by automobile. The one exception was when the three of them went on a cruise to the Caribbean.

To avoid detection during the boarding baggage check, Carmen scurried up the cruise liner's ropes. Then she joined Freddy and his wife in their cabin. It was a super-fun, memorable trip. They took loads of pictures which, naturally, showed Carmen peeking from the top of Freddy's shirt pocket.

Freddy's wife and Carmen were the best of friends. They spent a lot of time together, working in the garden, cleaning house, or merely chitchatting on the porch. They often would go shopping at the mall. When they did, Freddy's wife would tuck Carmen into her open handbag. Carmen would peer from inside of the lip of the bag at the many sights along the way.

When they stopped somewhere for lunch, usually in a booth at a fast food restaurant, Freddy's wife would place her open handbag on the table. Carmen would sit in the bag's wide opening as she munched on food handed to her by Freddy's wife.

Carmen's favorite food was chicken nuggets and French fries. She would surreptitiously dip broken in half fries and bits of nuggets into a small container of honey mustard sauce. Of course, Carmen would remain hidden inside the bag so that other patrons would not see her. As you know, mice are not allowed in restaurants.

Then, along came Freddy's first boy, Richard. After that the couple's first child, Angeline was born.

Then there were Tony and Shelly. Eddie was next, followed closely by Josh, then Jay, and finally Elizabeth - eight children in all! As the children grew older, they had many pets - dogs, cats, guinea pigs, birds, ducks, chickens, fish, even a goat. And, of course, they also had mice, white mice.

But the children's pet white mice were not special mice like Carmen, Peter, Charlie, Brutus and the sixteen other members of the troupe. The children's white mice couldn't talk. They just ran round and round in their upright exercise wheel.

Freddy's children tried to get their pet mice to talk, but the mice wouldn't make a noticeable talking sound. Even Carmen tried to teach the mice to talk. However, just like Freddy's children, all she got out of the white mice were the all too familiar mouse squeaks.

As the children grew older, their interests changed, from pets to games and sports to boys or girls and then to working outside the house. Eventually, one by one, the six children departed their mother and father's nest to strike out on their own. The house was suddenly quiet, too quiet.

Shortly after Elizabeth departed, Carmen decided that she should return to Australia to live with her relatives. Like Freddy, Carmen was getting along in her years. Her red hair had streaks of gray. Her reddish brown whiskers had long ago turned white. She had the customary aches and pains that come with aging. Moreover, she longed to work in the company of the human; Ariel-e is her name, who was directing the Aussie troupe.

As Carmen had mentioned to Freddy years ago, Ariel-e was very pretty. She had long brown hair and dark brown eyes. She was a terrific singer and her acting was unmatched by no other human Down Under. She was a huge success. She had made a few best-selling albums and was beginning to be known internationally.

She also worked with the mouse troupe in her spare time. She was an excellent adviser to the troupe and a good deal of fun. She even taught the members of the troupe how to roller skate! Ariel-e was surely the best roller skater around.

Thanks to Ariel-e, the mouse troupe was very successful. They performed night after night for adoring human audiences and, for sure, for admiring crowds of mice. They had thousands of fans Down Under.

But the troupe desperately needed a new bookkeeper. The troupe's bookkeeper, Camielle, longed to live in America and was preparing to leave the troupe. Camielle was Carmen's third cousin. Once she learned that Camielle was planning to quit the troupe, Carmen decided to return to her bookkeeping job as Camielle's replacement.

So it was - with a lot of tears and tender loving embraces, Carmen said goodbye to her best friend, her brother of sorts, Freddy. It surely was a sad day when Carmen left. Even today, Freddy really hasn't gotten over Carmen's going away. Thankfully, he has loads of pictures of Carmen. And, of course, he has even more fond memories. Since he is now single, the pictures and memories and happy times with Carmen and, of course, his children keep him going.

Carmen and Freddy exchange letters now and then and they always remember each other's birthdays. Carmen's is the seventeenth of June and Freddy's is the first of July. Ariel-e writes letters for Carmen. She posts them as well since mice are not supposed to be in post offices - at least not as legitimate customers. Carmen calls Freddy every Christmastime too. Naturally, she reverses the charges.

Then one day many years after Carmen had left, Freddy was walking past the family room where his four grandchildren were playing. There was loads of laughter, shrieks of joy, plenty of fun going on inside the room. Freddy smiled as he paused at the door to listen in.

He could hear Julian shouting over and over, "No way!" Then Micah would say, "I cannot believe this!" Gianna would giggle as she said, "This is too cool!" And Joy would laugh and laugh and laugh some more.

Then, oddly, he noticed that his grandchildren began to sing the Happy Birthday song.

Freddy thought about this for a moment. Whose birthday was it? Surely it wasn't someone's birthday in his immediate family. As far as he could recall, no one in his family was born on the third of March. He looked at the date displayed on his watch to make certain.

It was then that Freddy heard something out of the ordinary. There was another voice that he did not recognize that was coming from inside the room. It was a high-pitched female voice!

The voice had exclaimed exuberantly, "Thank you, I thank you very much. You're too sweet. This is the best birthday ever!" Then his Grandchildren were clapping their hands and laughing.

Freddy became overly alarmed. Thinking the voice belonged to one of his grandchildren's playmates, visiting without his knowledge and without permission from the child's parents, he knocked on the door.

"Kids, can I come in?"

"Sure, Grandpa Snickerdoodle," Julian yelled. "Come on in. The door is unlocked."

When Freddy opened the door, he saw that his grandchildren were sitting in a semicircle on the floor. Each of them had a big grin on his or her face. In front of the cheerful children, a mouse was sitting on her haunches. The mouse spun around where she sat to look at Freddy.

The mouse had darkish blond hair. Her stunning green eyes sparkled in the soft fluorescent light of the room. She was quite fair-skinned, well, I should say, furred, for a mouse. Surprisingly, she also had adorable freckles on her face!

Yes, you read that correctly. She had freckles! A few freckles also adorned her shoulders. Needless to say, she was exquisitely beautiful and quite unique for a mouse. She smiled at Freddy.

It was then, when she smiled, that Freddy noticed she had a darling dimple on the lower portion of the left side of her cheek. It was just below the crease of her lips. She was very attractive! And she looked very much like his wonderful mouse friend Carmen, but much younger. This mouse was perhaps fifteen years old or so.

She was wearing a pink dress with a matching pink hat. She had painted her nails a soft pink. Her delicately applied lipstick matched the color of her nails. She was - how had Carmen put it? She was *bare-pawed* since she was not wearing shoes on her hind paws.

As he stared at the mouse and she stared back at him in return, Freddy wondered.

Is this Camielle, the third cousin mouse of which Carmen spoke? If so, perhaps it was her voice that he heard outside the door.

Is it possible that there is more than one talking female mouse in the world of mice? He answered his own questioning thoughts by thinking to himself, this is wonderful! Another gorgeous talking mouse - Camielle!

"Hi, kids," Freddy said at last. He was sporting a big smile. "I see you have a new friend here. What's her name?" He chuckled, "Or haven't you named her yet?"

Micah said with a silly laugh, "Grandpa, she's just a mouse. Mice don't have names, you know that."

Micah, along with Freddy's three other grandchildren giggled.

Freddy looked around the room saying, "But I thought I heard someone else that was talking. Or maybe it wasn't someone; perhaps it was something."

He looked at Camielle, and then he said playfully, "Have you taught your mouse how to talk? Can she talk like my good mouse friend, Carmen?"

Freddy's grandchildren giggled once more. They looked at one another with amusement.

Then Julian, as he looked at Camielle, had said, "Grandpa, you know that mice can't talk."

The kids glanced at each other yet again, their giggles even more apparent.

With a serious look on his face, Micah said, "Remember that fairy tale you told us Grandpa, the one about the talking mouse, Carmen?"

"Well, yes I certainly do," Freddy said. "But it wasn't a fairy tale, Micah. It was a true story. Carmen and at least three other mice were truly able to talk. The mice that I heard talk, along with Carmen were Peter, Charlie, and Brutus."

Then, Gianna, her face beaming said, "Oh Grandpa, you're too funny! You know that mice cannot talk. We know that story about Carmen and the other talking mice was make-believe. You just made it up to entertain all of us. Besides, if mice could talk, they wouldn't talk to grown-ups. That's a law, Grandpa."

She looked at Camielle saying with caution, "That's a Mouse Kingdom law, Grandpa. Never, ever talk to human adults."

It was then that Freddy noticed that Camielle was nodding her head. Next, glancing over her shoulder to ensure that the children could not see her face, Camielle smiled and winked at Freddy.

Freddy smiled and winked in return. He was fairly certain that he knew what was going on. Certainly

Camielle could talk and she was most likely playing a game with the kids. The wink had confirmed it!

Just as he thought this, Freddy had an abrupt pang in his heart. He truly missed his lovely, redheaded best friend, Carmen. He missed her daily conversations with him a whole bunch. Yet, sitting on the floor was Carmen's third cousin, Camielle. She was just as pretty as Carmen, probably just as bold, all dressed up - and almost certainly just as loquacious and strong-willed!

"Well, okay then," Freddy said with a huge grin. "If you say so, I believe you. Then, pretending that he was looking around the room once more, he added, "Have fun with your mouse and behave yourselves. I'll call you down to supper shortly. Don't forget to wash your hands, okay?"

Freddy's grandchildren cried in unison, "Okay, Grandpa. We won't!"

Freddy turned to leave the room. Then he stopped to look at Camielle. With a big grin on his face, he added, "Especially after playing with mice!" He winked at Camielle and chuckled.

Camielle suddenly stood on her hind legs. She crossed her front legs across her chest and glared at Freddy for the longest time. Her right hind paw was thumping rapidly on the floor. She obviously learned that trait from Carmen. Then she burst out laughing and winked in return.

As Freddy closed the door behind him, he was in high spirits. He could hear renewed giggles and shouts of joy coming from the other side of the door. His darling grandchildren had a talking mouse for a friend. Perhaps Camielle would take turns accompanying each of them to school like Carmen had done with him. That would be loads of fun.

Just as he was about to walk down the hall, he heard Camielle say, "It'll be our little secret, at least for now. I'll eventually tell your Grandpa. But trust me; he's the only human adult I'll ever talk to. As you know, it's a Mouse Kingdom law - never ever talk to human adults!" She giggled.

"Now where was I? Ah, yes, about those other brown mice of the Aussie dance troupe. Well, there were Peter, and Charlie and oh! - there was this one stubborn mouse named Brutus…"

The End